Absolute Resolve

C.R. McBride

Part Two of The Coffee Café Series

Acknowledgments

I would like to thank as always my fellow author Caroline Easton for her ideas and company throughout. I would also like to thank my sister Andrea Busby and Pat Kerrell for proof reading and spell checking - a boring and tedious job that I cannot thank them enough for.

Also thanks to Julia Gibbs for giving both books a full proof read.

I also want to say a huge thanks to Chelsea Watmore whose encouragement and daily twitter chats have kept me writing xx

Other Titles by C.R McBride

Bitter Reflections

Happy reading xx

I would like to dedicate this book to my father who was taken from us in 2012. Cancer is a cruel illness and I urge everyone to help research and care charities in any way possible. Small amounts make amazing differences.

Happy Birthday, Dad xxx

Prologue

"SO?'' THE HOSTILE fat man asked abnormally calmly as a thin young man stood trembling before him, twisting his hands frantically. "What you are telling me is that a heavily pregnant woman climbed out of a tiny window, shimmied down a drainpipe and hotwired a car. Is that what you are trying to tell me, son? Is that really what you are trying to say?" His voice remained calm but there was no mistaking the threatening tone behind it.

"No, no of course not, I'm not saying that, Mr Thomson." The man quivered as he spoke, sweat dripping from his forehead.

"Good, good," he laughed. "Because, son, I would have to be a fucking moron to believe that load of bullshit, you little prick! Now tell me where the fuck she is!" he roared, the calmness he had displayed at first was gone and a furious temper replaced it. Two large men appeared and grabbed the small shaking man, striking him hard across the face. Mr Thomson rose from the seated position behind his overly large oak desk, and towered over the young man whose lip was now swollen and had a trickle of blood seeping from it. "We are not gonna fall out are we, son? Because I like you! Really I do, you have nothing to be scared of if you tell me the truth." He smiled and tapped him on the shoulder, staring intently into his eyes.

The young man had known this was going to happen, he had little hope that he would make it through this, but he would be damned if he was going to watch his boss kill that beautiful young woman. He had helped her, he had sneaked her out of the room where she had been held prisoner, helped her down the stairs and into a car that he had parked up earlier that morning. She had begged him tearfully to come with her, to escape together, but he had refused, knowing full well that Mr Thomson's men would notice them missing straight away if he had left with her. Together, they had no chance. If he stayed he could delay them, give her as much time as possible to escape, to get far away from this devil that now stood before him. He knew what would happen, knew he would be killed when they found out, but somehow that paled into insignificance when he looked at the beautiful woman's face, when he heard her singing that exquisite lullaby to her unborn. She had radiated a serenity he had never known, even in her dark dungeon where she knew she had no hope of survival, she had sung, and as she did his heart had sung with her. He had realised there and then that such an exquisite creature, an angel like her, should not, could not be taken from this world.

He sighed, "I don't know what happened, boss." Smack! Before the words had come out of his mouth, Mr Thomson had landed a punch himself. His fist was harder and heavier than the other men's, his hatred congregated in his hands.

"Fucking little prick!" he spat out at the young man, how dare this little runt, how dare he defy him? No one disobeyed him, he gave orders and people obeyed, if not, they did not live to regret it. "You have no idea how pissed off I am right now, I cannot allow her to live, do you understand me? Now tell me where the fuck she has gone!" As he continued to screech the other men in the room flinched a little, knowing full well how this was going to end. The fat man's face was now fire red, his fury flowing off him in waves, the young man was done for now and he knew it.

Confidence suddenly began to flow through his body as he realised he was facing death, he accepted his fate and felt strong and proud that he had managed to protect the beautiful angel from this evil.

"You are never gonna hurt her again you sick, selfish bastard!" he spluttered, and spat out the blood that was pooling in his mouth onto his boss's shoes, the room fell silent but the young man stayed defiant, staring his executioner straight in the face. Mr Thomson looked at his shoe in utter shock, no one had ever stood up to him before, he almost admired the boy for it but the feeling soon faded and he sighed heavily.

"Oh, son, you really shouldn't have done that!" He calmly reached into his pristine jacket and pulled out a gun that was nestled under his arm in a holster. Without blinking he shot the young man straight through the elbow. The young man howled out in pain, then let out another scream as his other elbow received the same treatment. "Feel like talking yet?" he asked, laughing emotionlessly. "Little prick, who do you think you are? What did you think I would do to you?" He strolled around the man who grasped his elbows in an attempt to stem the blood flow, reeling in agony on the floor. "Once more, where, is, she?" He emphasised his desire to retrieve the information by pressing his thumb hard into the hole he had created in the man's left elbow. The young man screamed, begging him to stop, nearly passing out from the pain that caused him to vomit on the carpet. Trying to catch his breath he stared through tear-soaked eyes, of all the evil things he had done in his short, misspent life he was not going to do this, he was not going to betray her. If he was meeting his Maker today, then maybe this honourable deed would exonerate him. Seeing the resolve in the young man's eyes, seeing that he was not going to relinquish any information, the boss muttered, "Oh fuck this!" and put a final bullet through the man's head.

Returning to his desk, he opened up his top drawer and coolly placed his gun down, gently straightening it up before closing it. He looked up at the two men who were standing stock still, stunned and now covered in the victim's blood. "I want her found, now, this very second, understand?" The two men nodded and turned to leave. "Well don't leave this piece of crap in here with me, you morons, get him out and clean this shit up, Jesus!" Why was he

always surrounded by idiots? he
thought to himself as the two men struggled, trying
to wrap the man up in the bloodstained rug,
dragging him out of the office. This was not
happening, he had worked too long and too hard to
let that little bitch ruin everything.

He rubbed his hands together as if trying to rub
away the blood that wasn't there. "Shit!" he hissed
out loud. She could end all of this, put him in prison,
how the hell did he let her get so close to him? She
was supposed to be just a distraction, a bit of fun,
how the hell was he to know she was a virgin? An
unprotected virgin. He had thought that his men had
dealt with her after he had got bored, hell it
wouldn't be the first time they had rid him of his
playthings, but no, she'd been dumped, then found
by a busy-body of a nosey Samaritan who had taken
her to hospital. They had no idea she was walking
around living and breathing, let alone pregnant. Sad
and lonely, the stupid girl had returned to her home
town to see her family, when his men had
unexpectedly seen her and dragged her back to him.
She had made threats, told them she had
information that would put them away but that it
was safe where they would never find it. Mr
Thomson had been livid, he couldn't kill her yet,
couldn't risk it until he was sure she was lying or
until he retrieved whatever it was that she had on
him. He had decided to keep her close where he
could watch her, and so she had been locked up in a
room in his own house, a tiny bedroom just down
the hall from his office. She had been locked up in

that tiny room for over a week and still not talked, not even a hint as to what she had on him. She was stronger than he had first thought; he had decided that she needed more persuasion to talk, when that little runt had decided to help her escape.

He had to find her, find her and this time deal with her properly. Maybe a price on her head was needed, he would make sure every lowlife in the country was out looking for her, she would have no chance and when he did find her, when he got his hands on her, he would threaten to cut that kid straight out of her womb, then she'd talk. He picked up his phone and made the call, she was not going to get far and when they found her he was going to make her pay.

The heavily pregnant woman had been driving for what seemed like hours but she dare not stop, she had stayed off the motorways and main roads for fear that they were looking for her already and if they were, what had happened to the poor man who had tried to help her? Oh God, she dare not think about it, Mr Thomson was a brutal and cruel man. Tears tumbled down her cheeks as she thought about her saviour's fate. That poor young man who had talked to her, tried to make her comfortable. He had often sneaked her food in and milk so the baby would grow strong. The lullabies that she had sung every night had not been for her baby but had been for that poor man who stood outside her door secretly listening. His boss was a fan of picking up young kids, training them so they were loyal and knew no other life. This man was no different but what the boss was doing to her did not sit well with the young man, and she saw day by day that he had a kind heart and wanted desperately to help her. When he had suggested escaping she had refused, these people were cruel and callous and would kill him if they found out he was the one who had helped her, but the man was adamant, he wanted her to live if not for herself, for the sake of her baby, she had to live through this. He had sacrificed himself for her child.

The woman's hand smoothed over her large stomach, trying to ease the pains that had steadily worsened over the last hour, she had to stop, but where? She had no idea where she was. She had just driven and driven for miles, needing to escape, and now as she desperately tried to find some sort of landmark through the torrential rain, the reality of her predicament hit home hard. The fuel light blinked rapidly but still she dare not stop, she was petrified of what Mr Thomson would do to her, not just her, what he would do to her precious child, because he had no heart or compassion. She had been devastated when she first realised that she was pregnant but as the baby grew she had felt it, connected with it. When her heart was just about to burst from the overwhelming hopelessness of her situation, locked away in that tiny prison, she would stroke her stomach and the baby would bounce around as though enjoying the touch. There was nothing evil about this unborn child, that monster may have created it but the child would know nothing of its father, of its past. She would make sure that the child would be brought up loved and cherished, and never know the horror its evil father had created around him.

She smiled at the thought of her beautiful baby happy and playing, just before crippling pain had her screaming out, she bent double, crying loudly, rendering her unable to control her car. She swerved violently off the road and ploughed into a ditch, crashing into the stone wall, the impact throwing her forward. Her head made a repulsive, crunching noise as it hit the steering wheel, shooting pain in her stomach caused her to sit back and cradle it desperately, trying to ease it. But then the contractions started again. "Oh God, it's too early," she cried out, frantically looking around for a house, a building, any sign of life, but all she saw was fields. Endless, green, fields. The contractions pulled her into a ball once more. "Please don't let me die!" she pleaded, "Please, someone help me!" The inevitable was happening, her baby was coming and there was nothing she could do, she was alone, in the middle of nowhere. For the first time she prayed to a God she had never before believed in. "Please let my baby survive, I know I have displeased you and made stupid mistakes through my life but please, God, save my innocent sweet baby." She looked down, weeping uncontrollably. She didn't even know if she was having a boy or girl, she had been too scared to go to the hospital for check-ups or scans but as she got close to giving birth she wanted to see her mother, hold her, have her tell her it was going to be alright. That never happened as Mr Thomson's men had snatched her before she got anywhere near her home, she would never see her mother again, never be able to say goodbye. Her mother would never know that she was pregnant, that she had a grandchild to love and spoil. She had run away from home as soon as she found out she was pregnant, fearing the disappointment her parents would feel. She had thought Mr Thomson would offer her a better life, a comfortable happy life, but she had been a blind fool.

Tears poured in torrents now and mixed with the blood that seeped from her forehead. They had beaten her badly that morning, kicked her stomach as she screamed defensively, trying to protect her unborn child. He had threatened to do much worse if she didn't start talking, she feared his temper, he was unstoppable and capable of things she didn't even want to contemplate. What if he had done something? What if he had hurt the baby and that was why it was coming early? The painful thoughts raced through her young fragile mind, despair flooding her. "Please, I know I didn't want my baby at first, I know I asked you to take it away but now it's different. I have grown to love my baby I can't ..." Another agonising scream left her lips and the contractions began to come quicker, "Please let my baby live, God, please send someone to be with us, don't let me die alone, I don't want to die alone." With that lasting plea still ringing in the air her waters broke, the urge to push took over, and she cried out painfully into the torrential, deafening rain.

Chapter 1

"MR MILL-THORPE, I can't tell you how much I loved your book." The girl leaned over the table smiling seductively as she passed her book over to him to be signed. She wasn't the first and he was pretty sure she wouldn't be the last, since his first novel had become popular these girls were all but throwing themselves at him.

"That's very kind, I so glad you enjoyed it, who would you like me to make it out to?" He plastered on his fake smile and tried not to flinch as she giggled, squeezing her chest together tightly and fluttering her long, purple eyelashes.

"I'm Tammy, you can add your number as well if you like!" Cue the fake, insincere smile!

Nick Mill-Thorpe's parents had died in a car crash when he was a baby, he had no pictures of them, no memories, he didn't even know their names. He had spent a short time in his teens trying to track down some sort of information but had no success. Adoption records are highly confidential and no one is allowed access to any of the information, but his seemed to be harder to find than any other of the children he had met over the years. All he knew was that they died, well, that he had been found in a crashed car, other than that there were simply no records. He was not put up for adoption before the crash so he was obviously wanted by them, it was just that fate had other plans. He felt no remorse though, his adopted mother and father were the most loving couple and had spoilt him since the day he had arrived, or so they told him anyway. They had worked in the theatre, where he remembered with great fondness the overwhelming sense of family that he always had with the troupe they travelled with. They were always friendly and always eager to take turns in watching Nick as his parents performed. Nick had been just a boy when his adopted father had died of a heart attack at the age of just thirty-eight years. Since his death, Nick's mother, Diane, had taken a backseat in the productions and whilst she continued to help out she never had the desire to return to the stage. Nick always wondered if she secretly missed the spotlight, as his mother never expressed her feelings towards it in front of her one and only child. Having experienced the pressure of it all lately, he doubted it.

"Mr Mill-Thorpe, I loved your book!" Another young girl and another pair of teenage breasts heaved in front of him. He turned to his agent, Melissa, and gave her the prearranged secret signal that told her he needed a break. She looked down the long line of girls, Jesus, each signing that he did, the line just got longer and longer. She moved her way down, counting ten girls then putting her hand out said:-

"Last one, ladies, then Mr Mill-Thorpe will be taking an hour long break." The sounds of disappointment echoed down the line as the news spread to those waiting outside, none of them, however, made a move to leave.

"You can't complain, Nick!" Melissa tried to reassure him as he stood taking three long puffs on his inhaler, "You have had amazing success with your first book. This success should be an author's dream! It so rarely happens, Nick."

"I know, I know." Nick heaved a sigh "Don't get me wrong, Melissa, I'm over the moon, I really am, it's just...I thought being a writer meant anonymity, you know being in the background. I don't like all this attention, I just can't get used to it." Melissa smiled sympathetically, understanding his reserve, he was a lovely man but he was painfully shy and riddled with self-doubt, but the truth was that he was a good-looking boy and his story had touched the hearts of most of the teenage girls in the UK.

"Nick, we need to face facts, you have to get used to all this attention, it will be magnified ten times over when the book is released in America. If we are going to get movie people interested you have to get out promoting, it is all part and parcel, sweetie." Nick looked at her gloomily. Melissa had been a rock for him, she was always looking out for him, only accepting things she knew he could handle, she went way beyond just an agent, she was his second mother, protecting him ferociously, and he loved her dearly, he wouldn't do anything to let her down. "Come on, two more hours and I promise I will get you out of here and straight into a quiet hotel room where you can order room service to your heart's content and just slob out!"

True to her word, after just two and a half hours Melissa was hustling him out of the door, much to the line of girls' displeasure. Nick now lay across a huge double bed with just his boxer shorts on, a beer in one hand and the TV remote in the other; she was indeed a real-life angel and this right here was his own personal heaven.

"Hey, Nick." Melissa entered cheerfully, unashamed at his lack of dress, her arms filled with flowers, chocolates and letters that had all been sprayed with perfumes of every kind, the smell was sucker-punching his senses as she plonked herself at the end of his bed.

"What the hell is all that?"

"Your ever-adoring fans have left piles of this stuff all over the foyer," Melissa giggled.

"Why?" Nick asked innocently, taking some of the burden from her.

"Oh bless you, they love you, Nick, they want to show you. I think the time has come that we might have to employ someone to deal with all this stuff for you...what the..." she trailed off as she opened a package, only to have a pair of knickers fall out into her lap. She jumped up like a rocket, causing all the letters and gifts to spray out all over the hotel room floor.

"Burgh," Nick cried out, "That's disgusting, what do I want a pair of them for?" Nick was outraged, Melissa just laughed.

"Remind me to tell you about some of the things we found in the packages when I used to work for larger agencies! You wouldn't believe what some of these woman send good-looking writers or actors!"

"Mm," Nick murmured, "I don't think I want to know."

"Look, not all of this stuff is from horny teenage girls, look read this one!" Melissa handed him a delicate, hand written note on lavender coloured paper:-

Dear Mr Nick Mill-Thorpe,

I know it's silly to write to you as you probably don't even open your own mail but I

just wanted to thank you personally for your wonderful book and tell you the impact it has had on mine and my daughter's life.

My daughter and I have been growing distant over the past few years, after her father and I separated, resulting in a nasty divorce. She decided to move out to live with her father and I thought I had lost her forever. I had never been alone before and so I began to read a lot to fill in the time I found myself with. My friend told me about your book and so I borrowed it from her and really enjoyed it. My daughter then came for a rare visit and saw it on the table, and we just got talking. She had read it too and told me all about her thoughts and views on it. It was the most animated conversation we'd had for ages. We have now joined your fan club online and talk over the site when we are not together.

I can't tell you how important my daughter is to me, and thanks to you I feel like she has returned to me. We found, through you, a connection again. We are planning to take a trip together to attend one of your book signings when you come over to Ireland. Until then I just wanted to let you know how wonderful your writing has been to me.

Thank you so much

Sharon

Melissa sniffled as she read it over his shoulder. "You see, that is what is important, your writing has touched that woman, made her reconnect – that's what's important, remember that." She rubbed her nose with her tissue. "I will leave you with the rest, shall I?" Nick just nodded, still holding the letter in his hand.

"Melissa!" he called out. "Make sure we send this woman something, books, photos, anything, and is there any chance we can get her a private invite to the signing thing so she can come straight up front?" Melissa agreed, without argument.

"Let me know if you get anything else gross!" she shouted as she shut the door behind her.

One by one Nick began to open the letters; yes, most of them were girls telling him how much they loved him, or giving him their telephone numbers, there were even a few naked photographs! But in amongst all the plastic, fake attention seekers, there were a handful of letters that were amazing. They told him how they had been through the same things as the characters had in his story, how they felt as though he was speaking to them directly and that how his little book, his little story had changed their lives. He got up off the bed, allowing the envelopes to fall around his bare feet, sat down at the desk and began writing. If these girls and women had taken the time to write to him, then by God he was going to take the time to write back, it was the least he could do to thank them personally.

Chapter 2

NICK SHRUNK UNDER the blankets as Melissa threw the curtains back allowing the blinding sun to stream into the room

"For fuck's sake, Melissa!"

"Oh well, that's nice talk on a gloriously beautiful summer morning," she sang out, unperturbed with his foul language, Nick just groaned and tried to disappear further down the bed. "Don't even start with that, Nick," she scolded ripping the duvet off the bed "You have interviews all day, get up, get dressed and get out there!"

The dirty look that Nick threw her said everything he needed to say, he was NOT a morning person and absolutely hated the way Melissa was all bright eyed and bushytailed the minute her alarm went off. "Coffee," he grunted.

"You don't even drink coffee, Nick, now get up!"

"Maybe I need to start drinking it if you are gonna drag my arse out of bed at this time every morning!"

"Stop being a baby."

"Stop treating me like a baby."

"Stop acting like a baby, then."

"Stop….stop… oh I can't be arsed."

Melissa shook her head as Nick shuffled off into the bathroom, God, she loved him so much. Nick had been a timid young man when his mum had introduced them. Through her work in the theatre Nick's mum had a lot of contacts among agents and producers, even many actors, but never told Nick that and never used them to help him out. Her Nick needed to make it on his own and he would not thank her for trying to help him. When she found out that Melissa had left her old firm of agents, she had called her and asked if she would be interested in popping round for dinner. Melissa had nothing else planned so had called round to the house to meet them. She had known the family for years as her firm represented a number of actors that did theatre work. Since Nick's Uncle George seemed to entertain all of the theatre troupes, everyone knew Nick's mum and, therefore, also knew Nick. Nick had been a gangly looking man back then. He had finished university and had a few jobs, but felt writing was his passion. Up until that point he had only written as a hobby, but as soon as Melissa read his story she knew exactly what his mother had been up to. The way Nick's writing captured her heart was unique, of course he refused to believe that he was anywhere near good enough to be published, but Melissa and his mother had persisted. Melissa had begged him to let her read his work, after a carefully and precisely placed unsuspicious comment from his mother brought up the subject of his writing. It had taken two months to persuade

him to let anyone else read it, then
longer to get him to allow them to get it published.
Now here they were, an instant hit. Melissa had
hoped that, having just celebrated his twenty-sixth
birthday, Nick might have grown up more and stood
up to the pressures of a public life; that, however,
was not proving to be the case, he just shrank away
from cameras and fans. He was talented, and Melissa
was going to make sure that he was protected and
she would not allow him to be bullied into doing
things he did not want to do, she took baby steps
with Nick.

Nick looked at his reflection as he stepped out of
the shower; yes he was tall and had dark hair and
true, since he had joined the local gym his body was
beginning to take on shape, but really he was no oil
painting in his opinion. What did all these girls see
in him? They would scream at him, hand him phone
numbers and now they were sending him their
knickers! It was surreal, beyond weird and quite
scary sometimes. He never had women chasing him
before he was famous, they would call him 'sweet' or
'such a good friend', never had they wanted to date
him. The inhaler that he produced often was a
definite turn off, everyone told him he would
probably grow out of his need for an inhaler, that he
just had a childhood form of asthma but he had
never grown out of it. If anything, the attacks had
increased, causing pains in his chest and a
numbness he couldn't describe. The minute fame
had hit, he suddenly became irresistible to these
women, so what was so different now? They were

not interested in him, they just wanted the fame he brought them and some of them were so young it was embarrassing. Young girls were dressing up so provocatively to come to his signings and the mothers were letting them, he just didn't understand.

The last thing he needed right now was to get involved with a woman, he had tried to have relationships before but they never worked out. Melissa yelling through the door shook him from his thoughts, he dried himself and went to get dressed.

"Please tell me you are not planning on wearing that thing!" Melissa gasped as Nick joined her for breakfast.

"What's wrong with it?" Nick stood looking down at his favourite jumper. He was doing a radio interview, so why did he have to get dressed up?

"You look like you're going fishing, Nick, that's what! For goodness sake! Get it off!"

Nick pouted. "I love this jumper."

"OFF! NOW!" Sometimes his childishness really tried her temper.

"Fine." Nick stripped it off and sat down to breakfast, bare chested and grinning. "Happy now?"

Melissa tried in vain to hide her amusement. "Funny," she said sarcastically, "Drink your tea."

"Yes, my agent mummy."

"Carry on, and I will call your mother and tell her what a sulky child you are being," she threatened.

"OK, OK." He held his hands up in surrender, laughing fondly, not wanting another lecture from his mother. "So what's on the menu today?"

Melissa ran through the day's interviews and events with him; "few magazine interviews, they will be basic girly questions, what's your favourite colour? Favourite film? etc. etc. usual stuff, then there's that one," she pointed to a book magazine "That one wants to talk to you about which books influenced you as a child and what you are reading now!" Reading now! Were they kidding, when did he have time to read?

"What are you reading?" he asked Melissa as he shoved half a slice of buttered toast into his mouth.

"Erotica!" she smirked. "Would you like the title and author?"

"Ha ha, very funny! Well if you're not going to help me," he mumbled, his mouth still full of the toast.

"Look, just go online and look to see if there are any books you fancy, and I will have them brought up, then at least you can say you've just started them." She continued down the list. "Last of the day is the radio interview with Dave Glinson." Nick groaned. Dave Glinson was 'all about the gossip, who needed the truth when you could make it up', sort of person.

"Why do I have to do an interview with him? He does movie stars and singers, why would he want to interview a first time author?"

Melissa rolled her eyes. "Do you realise how popular your book is becoming, everyone is talking about it, authors are rapidly becoming the new rock stars!" She noticed the worry on his face. "Don't worry, I will get a list of questions that he wants to ask you beforehand and tell him your personal life is a no-go area, OK?" She ruffled his hair affectionately. "Come on, sausage, let's get you into something more appropriate that doesn't make you look like you are going tuna fishing!"

"So who is your favourite singer?" the young girl asked, gazing up at him. She had short brown hair, shaved at the side, and her top was all but see-through. Her eyes could not be seen under the immense mascara and false eyelashes that hooded them. For four hours he had sat through the same questions, tried to be polite, tried to be honest, but really none of this was important. Who cared how he kept in shape? Or whether he was on a diet? Or worst still was, "Do you have a girlfriend at the moment?" He just wanted to talk about his book, what inspired him to write the story, where the ideas came from, but no one was interested. Even the interview with the book magazine was dull, he had started to talk about his childhood books but they had deviated, asking him whether he thought sex was appropriate in young adult reads! What sort of discussion was that to have? He did not have any sex in his book; well, a small bit but nothing graphic or explicit, so why were they asking him this? By the time they got around to talking about his actual story they had run out of time, then asked if they could get some pictures and would he mind undoing his shirt – talk about hypocritical.

"Mr Mill-Thorpe?"

"Oh sorry, I don't really get time to listen to music much, I do like a lot of songs but don't really follow anyone in particular." Ha! That should please Melissa, a non-committal answer.

"Could you name any songs then?" she continued.

Damn. "Well I grew up in the theatre so a lot of the songs I really love are from musicals and plays. I remember watching my mum and dad on stage singing together, it was amazing. The people I grew up with were all theatrical, and so our house was always filled with singing and stories".

The girl looked at him blankly, his story and joy of describing his childhood was lost on her so he just ran off a few pop songs that he had heard in the car on the way over. After this torture was the interview he was dreading the most, the radio interview with the repulsive Dave Glinson.

"You need to eat something, Nick," Melissa all but pleaded with him after he had finished his interview with the young girl. "It will be OK, I promise"

Nick nodded gloomily, they were seated in a tiny restaurant that Melissa had found round the back of the radio station. It matched his mood perfectly, the dull lighting left the room dark so no one could see any distance, therefore removing the risk of being spotted, shadows bounced off the walls making everyone unrecognisable. He picked at the pasta in front of him, his stomach churning over and over again, he just didn't have the nerve to do this. Melissa kept telling him that all the fuss surrounding him would die down and that things would not be this bad all the time, but the opposite was happening, the interest in him was just growing and it made him feel very uncomfortable. "I need a drink," he announced.

"I don't think that's a good idea, do you?" Melissa became concerned, Nick drank alcohol, yes, but he never felt the need for it or drank to excess.

"Yep, as a matter of fact I do, I need to take the edge off my nerves." With that he ordered a beer and drank the whole bottle down in one. This was not good, Melissa watched as he ordered another, maybe she should cancel the interview, no, that would be no good, Dave would just make up a load of rubbish to get back at them, no, she had to sort Nick out as best she could, try to get his nerves under control and get him into that studio.

Nick walked into the studio like a man walking down death row, his head hung and he failed to make eye contact with any of the staff. Melissa tried to apologise, stating he had had a long day of interviews, but the staff just raised their eyebrows, looking him up and down. He was ushered into his seat and Melissa was bustled out, panic set in as he was separated from her and dread filled his soul. The studio was small, tiny in fact. Nick sat in front of Dave, and Melissa was with two other producers behind a glass window. He felt alone, thrown to the wolves.

"So Nick, can I call you Nick?"

"Erm yeah, that is my name after all."

"It's just with a name like Nicholas Mill-Thorpe I feel like I should call you sir!" A rumble of laughter rippled round the studio.

"Nick is fine." He tried his best to sound calm and confident and hide the terror he really felt.

"So, forgive me if I move further round the table, beer and Italian for lunch, I am guessing from the smell of garlic! Do you always drink this early, Nick?" Melissa let out a long exasperated sigh, Nick scrunched his hands into a ball, calm and polite, that's what Melissa always told him, calm and polite.

"Only when I am celebrating being on a show as huge and popular as yours." Dave smirked at Nick's rebound.

"Greasing all the right poles eh, Nick!" he sneered, then taking a deep breath changed tone and cheerfully announced, "OK, we are going to play another song and then get straight back to Nick to ask him about his long term relationship with the beautiful Tanya and how he viciously broke her heart! Back in two."

Nick looked at Melissa, panic strewn across his face, Melissa was in a furious argument with one of the show's producers, she was frantically waving the list of pre-set questions in his face. "Shit," he cursed into his hand as he ran it across his chin, this was gonna be hell. Dave noticed the sign of defeat, this was his kingdom, he was king and if there was one thing he hated it was stuck up rich kids like this one in front of him. He was going to destroy him and he was going to enjoy doing it.

"Nick, slow down," Melissa called out as Nick practically ran from the taxi into the hotel lobby. "Nick, listen to me!" She caught the lift doors and slid in next to him.

"What the fuck was that? Who the hell is Tanya?" he roared, grabbing his inhaler from his pocket and taking two long hauls on it.

Melissa took a breath and spoke as calmly as she possibly could, with a furious man screaming in her face. "It seems some girl who went   to school with you sold her story to the press, told them you dated and that you broke her heart!"

"How?" Nick asked quietly.

"Pardon?"

"How did I supposedly break her heart?"

Melissa paused, looking at the seriousness of his face. "Slept with her friend," she muttered.

Nick rubbed his temples with both hands. "Well that's just fucking great, isn't it!"

"It's not that bad, look, that's it now for this week, have an early night and..."

"And what, Melissa? Everything will be alright in the morning? Bollocks!" he shouted, making her retreat to the back of the lift.

They rode the rest of the floors in silence. Melissa frantically tried to think of something to say but failed, Nick was a good kid; he prided himself on his manners and reputation. In one fell swoop this vicious girl had taken that away from him. He knew that his mother would be devastated, and that's what would be hurting him the most. Melissa made a note to herself that she would sue that 'cow' and make her pay for this, her and the radio station. What had she been thinking, booking Nick onto that garbage show anyway? She could kick herself. The truth was, she knew exactly why she had booked him on that show, Nick's target audience were teenagers, young adults and that was exactly who listened to that show. Maybe Nick just wasn't cut out for public life, but how the hell could she market him without a public face?

"I know it's not you, Melissa," Nick practically whispered as they reached his door, but still he couldn't look at her.

"I will sort it, I promise," she declared confidently. "I will not let anything like this happen again, I will sort everything out from now on. No more surprises!" She then tried to kiss him on his forehead, which was quite a feat for a little woman like her. Nick couldn't help smiling as she struggled to balance on her tiptoes and, taking pity on her, leaned down allowing her to complete the tender, affectionate gesture. His smile broadened a little and he opened his door but very quickly faltered at the sight of a naked girl with long blonde hair and big blue eyes lying across his bed. He turned to look at Melissa and taking her hand, he led her to the edge of the bed; the girl stared at Nick, speechless at finally realising her dream to sleep with 'The Nick Mill-Thorpe'.

"No more surprises, eh? You're going to sort everything out! Well, Melissa, you're in luck." He pointed to the girl, his eyes never leaving Melissa's. "Sort that!" He then turned and slammed the door behind him, leaving Melissa flabbergasted at the audacity of this girl, and a very confused naked girl who was about to feel Melissa's wrath.

Chapter 3

"IT'S NOT FUNNY, Uncle George!" Nick protested as his uncle lay on the sofa laughing so hard he was fighting for breath. After discovering the girl in his hotel room, there was only one place of security he wanted to go to. Uncle George offered a haven whenever Nick needed it. It did, however, have a downside and that was Uncle George himself! "It's serious; she could have been under age or anything!"

Uncle George drew a deep long lungful of air, gasping, "You're right, my boy, you're right, but come on, it is a bit funny I mean how many authors do you know have naked girls breaking into their hotel rooms! Then stripping off and just lying there, waiting for them to walk in and sweep them off their feet!" His face was bright red and he was stifling another chortle. Nick sighed, exasperated with the man. "What was she thinking? Oh, I will strip off, sleep with him and he is bound to ask me to marry him!" George let out another howl at his own amusement; Nick was not impressed. "Was she at least good looking?" Uncle George tried to lighten Nick's mood.

"I don't know, I didn't really look!"

"You didn't even... let me get this straight, she is lying there naked, like totally starkers, and you didn't even look!" Uncle George was aghast. "Not that it's any of my business, Nick, but are you? ... You know...not that it matters."

"George!" Nick blurted out. "I can't believe you just asked me that, just because I don't ogle people like you do. Just because I didn't look, doesn't automatically make me gay! It was humiliating for her and me, for God's sake, George, she is someone's daughter!" Uncle George now had that beaming smile ear to ear.

"Quite right, Nick, quite right! Besides, didn't really think you would join our ranks, my boy!" and once again his big booming laugh bounced around the lounge.

Uncle George was the brother of Nick's mother. He was a short, very round man with a huge personality. He had acted in the theatre with his mother, and sometimes forgot that he was not on a stage when he was talking and therefore did not need to speak so loud in general conversation. Most people would tell Nick to carry earplugs whenever they were going out with him, Nick adored him. When he was young George would perform at the drop of a hat and have Nick squealing in delight. It also meant that due to George's lack of desire to settle down with one man, Nick had a never-ending supply of step-uncles also eager to entertain; with Nick's father gone, he was only too happy to have all this male attention.

"Come on, I think a night out is called for, cheer us up. What do you say, Nick?"

"I think you've had enough entertainment out of me for one night!" Nick complained but he was already getting his jacket on, Uncle George had never been one for taking no for an answer.

"Mum's the word, I promise, my boy, all is good with the world."

Two hours later Nick and his uncle were seated in a local Italian restaurant, a regular haunt for all George's theatre pals.

"And so she was just lying there, naked!"

"Yes! He just walked in there and she was waiting for him." The whole table erupted again making Nick want to disappear, so much for keeping quiet.

"Nicky, my dear boy, that must have been awful for you." One of George's friends held his hand in an attempt to comfort him.

"How would you know, Billy? You've never even seen a woman naked!" George let out another roar of laughter; the others joining him, his friend just frowned.

"I don't have to have seen one, 'Mr- I'm- oh- so- experienced, I can appreciate the situation, poor Nick'." Nick smiled.

George's friends really were the loveliest bunch you could imagine, he adored spending time with them. After his father had died Nick had found himself cocooned in a web of love by Uncle George, he immediately stepped into a fatherly role without a second thought, and whilst Nick had missed his father terribly at the time, he never went without a thing emotionally or financially, Uncle George saw to that.

"Anyway, let's change the subject," Billy squeaked out. "We've hardly seen you since your book became a hit, how is it all going? Are you OK? Have you met any famous people yet?" Upon that question, the table suddenly hushed down, all of them waiting on Nick's answer. Nick chuckled. "No, no one famous not yet." At their disappointed looks, he added that he was due to go to several awards ceremonies so was bound to run into a few, maybe he could wangle some tickets for all of them, he was sure that Melissa would be able to sort something out for him. Billy jumped up and down excitedly in his seat; George gave him a stern look.

"We are theatre people, we do not associate with fly-by-night movie or even worse TV people." He stuck his nose in the air.

"Oh shut up, you pompous old queen, we are all one now, movie and TV stars love doing theatre and don't you dare try to tell me, George Mill, that you wouldn't bite the hand off a baboon for a spot in a movie, because I know you too well!" Nick nearly spat out the pizza that he had just taken a mouthful of, George sat aghast, his mouth wide open at Billy's outcry.

"A baboon's hand?" George echoed, as Nick collapsed as tears of laughter streamed down his face. "A baboon's hand?" he roared loudly, causing everyone in the restaurant to turn and stare at them. Billy just blew him a kiss nonchalantly and continued to delicately eat his salad. George looked around the table at all his friends hooting. "A bit harsh," he muttered under his breath "...a squirrel's maybe..." That was it, Nick's pizza went down the wrong hole and he spluttered and coughed until he could clear it. The whole table burst into laughter once more. and that was how it was with George and his friends. They never stopped laughing, always saw the funny side of everything and whilst it had been horrendous as a child, now it was quite relaxing. All the horrible things that happened George would turn into a humorous anecdote, and that would be it, it would be out in the open and no longer a problem.

"Thought those scrounging lot would never leave," Uncle George huffed as he cleared away all the glass tumblers that now littered his lounge floor, of course everyone had returned to George's after the restaurant as usual. He had always had an open door policy, everyone welcome at any time. It had driven his mother mad when they lived with him and was the main reason she had finally sought her own place, a small apartment across town. It had proved to be the making of her. She had found her independence and slowly but surely she had begun to live life again. Nick missed his father greatly but he loved Uncle George, and life was certainly never dull or boring when he was around. As a child it had been a wonderland, different people coming and going, hundreds of uncles and aunts calling in, bringing him toys and presents. Nick had thought it was the greatest place in the world and he had never wanted to leave. It was also never private!

"Right, time to break out the decent stuff, I think!" George unlocked a small cupboard and took out a bottle of brandy with two glasses. He poured out a small drop and handed the overly large glass to Nick, who was already glassy eyed at this point. He certainly didn't need any more alcohol, let alone very expensive and probably lethal alcohol. Nick was definitely going to regret this in the morning but no one ever said no to George, he simply didn't hear the word. "Your dad would have been so proud of you, Nick, you know that, don't you," George said, his voice suddenly very sombre.

"I'd like to think so," Nick replied, slowly swirling the bronze coloured liquid round and round his glass.

Uncle George slowly sat next to him on the sofa, which for a man George's size was not an easy task, all sorts of noises left his mouth as he lowered himself down. Nick grinned and shuffled along, allowing him more room. "I don't think, I know, Nick, your dad wanted the best for you, you were always going to be OK financially, if only that bloody mother of yours would let me spend more money on you now and again." He paused to take a sip from his own sparkling crystal tumbler, "...anyway more than anything he just wanted you to be happy. Are you happy, Nick?"

"I know, I am, I am doing really well. Honestly, Uncle George, I'm OK." George shook his head.

"Not OK, I didn't ask if you were OK, I asked are you happy?"

Nick stared into his glass, he had never been able to hide anything from George, never could, never would. "It's hard, George, you know that."

"I do, my boy, that's why I'm asking."

"There's a lot of commitments, pressure, it's not that I'm ungrateful, it's just...weird...it's hard with all these young girls around me all the time, I just feel a bit...I don't know.."

"Suffocated?" George offered. Yes, that was it, that was exactly how he felt, so consumed with everyone and everything around him he just couldn't breathe. George reached across and held Nick's hand. "Nicky, I have known you since you were a boy, I loved you before you were even born." Nick screwed his face up in a disgusted way. "Shut up, I don't care what you say, I have. But you are not coping and this is only going to get worse. You are talented, my boy, and you are going to go from strength to strength." He paused to take another slow sip of the brandy. "It takes time, all this attention, it takes a while to get used to, you know when Billy got offered that leading part, the one where he played a mad vicar, the first time he was asked for an autograph he pissed himself – literally pissed on the spot." George bellowed out the last part.

"George, don't be such a bitch," Nick chastised.

"I'm sorry, it was funny, though. Anyway, what your mother and I think is that you need a break, time away to reflect and just chill for a bit, what do you think?"

Nick thought for a moment, he had been nonstop since the book launch and had been travelling all over the country for months, would they let him take a break?

"I don't know, George, I have so many commitments and I don't think they would just let me disappear off for a...whoah. What are you doing? ...George? ...George?" George had picked up Nick's phone off the table and was dialling, oh God what was he doing? Did he not realise that it was two o'clock in the morning? He made a move to grab his phone but George was a large man and it was difficult to stretch over his rounded tummy to grab it. George heaved himself up and moved into the bathroom. "George, George, open this door and give me my phone back. Mum is going to be so pissed with you if you are calling her, George!" He banged on the door, it was useless, George was on a mission.

Half an hour later George emerged from the bathroom grinning, Nick had passed out face down and was sprawled across the sofa, his legs dangling half off, hanging over the edge.

"Lightweight," George whispered as he covered him with a blanket, "What did you do, just black out and fall onto the sofa in this position?" He smiled at him tenderly, then took a piece of paper off the desk and wrote Nick a note:-

Dearest Boy,

Your mother is worried and that means I'm worried, I called Melissa – oh was she mad at me, did you know what time is was? You should have told me – anyway she says she is going to clear a gap in your schedule. It won't be for a few months but she understands and was actually thinking the same thing. I have my cottage in the Dales that I never use, Billy went there last year, hated it, nothing goes on there, said it was really boring. To be honest I was going to put it on the market but it seems it would be a perfect retreat for you at the moment. Might have to do some cleaning up, no one's been there since. Some friends recommended this quiet village and so I bought it for when I was writing, but I never write anymore so it's redundant. Don't wake me up when you leave, call me when you're free and I will get you the keys and directions.

Love you

Uncle G

P.S Do not throw up on my Persian rug, there is a bathroom! I tell you, I wonder if you really are a Mill-Thorpe at times, you have no stamina!

George smiled as he placed the letter on the table in front of Nick, he really was a sweet boy and he was so proud of him. Since his father's death George had not hesitated to step in as a surrogate father figure, sometimes he forgot that Nick wasn't his own son. He had watched this vibrant, excited boy slowly turn self-conscious and completely stressed out, yes, a break was exactly what he needed. Melissa had not been happy at all when he called. Who knew women could swear like that, but hey, she had calmed down and agreed. The least he could do was offer his little cottage to Nick, hell, he couldn't even remember the last time he had been there, it was one of those insane, on-a-whim sort of things that led him to buy the cottage. One of his directors had talked about having a retreat and it sounded a great idea to George, so he had spoken to some friends who ran a wine bar and restaurant who recommended a little village in the Dales. At the time he had thought it was a fabulous idea, he would have peace and quiet and nothing but time to write plays, but in reality he loved the spotlight, loved being the centre of attention. Just two hours at the cottage had driven him to distraction, and he had come straight home and never been back since. He loved the people there, the funny little characters he had met in the pub but it was too quiet, too isolated and he felt claustrophobic, so had left. It was just rented out to friends and business acquaintances now. But Nick, he would love it, peace and quiet, anonymity was just what he needed right now.

George kissed his own fingers and placed them to Nick's forehead; he stirred a little but didn't wake. "Love you," George whispered, then grasped his glass and took himself off to bed.

Chapter 4

MELISSA HAD OUTDONE herself, after a lot of rushing around and rescheduling she had condensed all his commitments into just one and a half months. It had been hard work and Nick was wiped out, but somehow the thought of the isolated cottage kept him going and he actually began to relax a little and enjoy the attention, knowing that soon he would have nearly a month all to himself. A press release had been compiled, thanking everyone and advising that Nicholas Mill-Thorpe would be taking a break to allow him time to write a sequel to his bestselling book. It seemed to make them all happy knowing a sequel was on its way, and the press backed off a little. As he threw his bags into the back of his rented car, it seemed strange not having press on his doorstep taking photographs of his every move. He guessed he became less interesting when they knew he was not going to be doing anything but write for a while. It did, however, mean that he could safely escape without anyone knowing where he was staying and that was definitely appealing.

"Map – check, money – check, bags – check." Nick ran through his list out loud, ensuring that he had everything he needed. He had programmed his navigation 'thingy' in the car but it didn't like the address and was just directing him to the nearest town, so George had given him instructions over the phone.

"Are you being funny?" Nick had asked him as he wrote down the details George was relaying to him over the phone. George just laughed.

"Trust me; you will see when you get there."

"George, you haven't been there for years, but you're telling me to turn left by the row of parked cars! What if there are no cars parked there anymore? What if that road doesn't exist anymore? Towns do change, you know, they grow and develop!"

George had assured him that nothing ever changed around there, and to trust him because he would understand when he got there.

The relief of finally getting away soon faded into boredom, driving up the motorway was dull, dull, dull. Nick had forgotten to bring any form of music with him and so the only noise available was the constant, drone of the tyres on tarmac, interrupted intermittently by the occasional thud as he hit the cats' eyes in the middle of the road. It had been a long time since Nick had actually driven himself anywhere. Studios and interviews always sent cars to pick him up, and George always insisted on alcohol-based activities so taxis were required. To finally sit behind the wheel was alien and Nick found himself drifting, unable to drive in a straight line.

The houses and buildings that flew past his vision soon disappeared and were replaced with huge mounds of earth or grassy hills blocking the view, and so Nick was left counting down the junctions till he reached the one he needed. Deciding he needed a break, he pulled into a service station to get a coffee, it was nearly lunchtime, maybe he would grab a sandwich also. He found a seat and took a sip of his hot, steaming coffee, looking up over his cup he realised he was being watched. Oh please, not more fans, his heart sank but surely not, the couple staring were an elderly couple, he smiled and the old lady leaned over the talk to him.

"I'm sorry, dear, were we staring?" she called out over the tables

Nick chuckled. "It's OK, thought I might have spilled my coffee or something," he joked checking his top for stains as he spoke.

"We are awful, aren't we, we were just having a bet you see, he thinks you are a businessman but I thought you were going home to family, I was trying to see if you had a ring on!" Her husband elbowed her, hard.

"Shut up, Elsie, you are so nosey, I'm so sorry," the husband apologised. Nick smiled.

"Just getting away for a while, city life and all that," he explained. Elsie smiled and began to tell him that a lovely man like him should be going home to a lovely girl, was he married? Attached? Courting? Always the answer was no. She seemed sad at this and as they stood to leave she placed a hand on his shoulder. "Life has a habit of passing you by, you know, if you are not careful you will miss it." And with that she and her husband went, leaving Nick feeling depressed and not in the slightest bit hungry anymore!

Turning into the main town Nick now understood what Uncle George had meant, it was like stepping back in time, the houses were all stone, all with beautiful gardens and immaculate paintwork. Driving through the town (if that's indeed what it was) felt a million miles away from the city. The little high street was cobbled and full of tiny shops, none of which Nick had ever heard of, they all had tiny little doorways and dressed bay windows. He turned left and did indeed find a row of parked cars, then right at a bench that had seen better days, and straight on past the tree that looked like it was broken in the middle. Nick laughed out loud, how could all these landmarks still be the same years after George had visited? The cottages themselves now began to dwindle to the odd one as Nick went further and further into the Dales, and the countryside opened up before him, it was beautiful and breathtaking. The fields were all scattered randomly, and were different sizes with jagged edges like a homemade patchwork quilt of greens and yellows and browns. Each section stitched together with a crumbling dry stone wall dotted with the occasional tree. The road he drove on weaved in and around each field, and he slowed down to a crawl, opening all the cars windows so that he could enjoy the full effect of this amazing scenery. The rush of fresh air felt like he had just stepped out of an invigorating shower, his lungs deeply devouring the clean air hungrily.

Unbeknown to him there was a queue of traffic behind, and as he gazed at the sights they were rapidly losing patience, a loud horn blast caused Nick to look in his mirror; feeling panicked he pulled into the side and allowed the irate drivers to pass.

"Bloody tourists!" a man shouted out as he passed, the other car drivers threw him equally dirty looks as they crawled past then zoomed off into the distance, looking more like a train of rally cars than a stream of traffic. Letting out a long sigh he rested his head on the steering wheel, he'd only been here two minutes and had already upset the locals. A noise to the left of him startled him; a huge cow leant over the stone wall and leaned in through the open window, munching loudly. Its long shaggy ginger hair obscured its eyes but its enormous white horns were very visible. Nick held his breath, what the hell do you do in this situation? He couldn't drive off because the cow or bull's head was actually in his car. The horns, thank goodness, were far too large to fit in through the window but remained very visible, poking out from either side. Oddly though, he wasn't frightened, despite the sharp and harmful looking horns the beast seemed placid enough. Slowly, so as not to spook it, he gently reached out his hand and placed it on the beast's nose, scratching the long hair slightly. The beast seemed to like this and then without warning its long sticky tongue came out and licked up Nick's arm, leaving a long trail of grass covered goo as it did. "Yuk," he cried out and rapidly pulled his arm away, the beast not happy with his reaction to its obviously affectionate gesture pulled his head out of the car and went back to grazing. Nick was now left with a view of the creature's backside in his window. He desperately tried to find a cloth to wipe his arm but had to settle on shammy leather, smearing the saliva further up his arm. He then tried to pick off the bits of grass that were cementing themselves as they baked in the sun's rays, he would need a good shower when he got to George's cottage. Sighing loudly, he put the car into gear and continued on, following George's bizarre instructions.

After what seemed to Nick to be an endlessly long road, he finally passed a small sign that indicated he had reached the tiny village; he still had yet to see anything that resembled a village at all. He had passed a few farms, and turning right at the broken gate (another fabulous landmark from George that unbelievably was still there), the road had changed from tarmac to grey stones more like gravel. His paintwork took a pounding as the chips pinged off his doors and bonnet; thank goodness Melissa had sorted out full cover on this lease car. As he reached the top of the hill, the little village appeared before him. Clustered together in the middle of the patchwork surroundings were maybe twenty buildings and houses, all yellow/cream stone with brown roofs. Some had green ivy or roses covering them, clinging and climbing right up to the tops, delicate pink roses sporadically blossoming amidst all the green leaves. It was like a picture postcard of countryside life. Running alongside the road was a twisting, sparkling stream, not very deep but fast, with ripples and bumps where the water had to negotiate round boulders and banks. There was a stone arched bridge crossing it that allowed him to drive into the village, like a drawbridge over a castle moat. "This is where the fun begins," he muttered aloud because although George's directions had been spot on so far, there were no street names here, no house numbers, no markings to indicate where he was or where he was going. George had suggested stopping off at the pub and getting directions from there, as he was a little vague as to how to get to the cottage itself once he was over the bridge.

Nick pulled up outside 'The Horse Hoof House' pub, it wasn't hard to find as it was the only house that was bright white with a red tiled roof, hopefully they could direct him. Inside was like stepping through a time warp, the walls were stark white with wooden panelling, each wall covered in pictures, drawings, paintings and horseshoes. Along the tops of the walls were plate racks with different heavily patterned plates lined up all the way round the whole pub. The place fell silent as Nick entered, and all eyes turned to stare.

"Erm hi," Nick spoke intrepidly, and began feeling like he had walked into a horror movie. "I was wondering if anyone could help me find Pine Tree Cottage?" *Anyone who isn't a werewolf or vampire,* Nick thought to himself as the suspicious stares continued. There were a number of grumbles from around the room; George had thought this name was funny as there was not a pine tree in sight round here, but it seemed the locals did not share his sense of humour. From behind the bar a young woman spoke out.

"You want our help but you're not even gonna buy a drink?"

"Of course, I was just heading up there now," Nick said shamefully, all eyes still followed him as he stepped up. It was safe to say that the woman behind the bar definitely stood out from the crowd, whilst everyone in the pub wore jumpers, jeans or boiler suits she would not have looked out of place in the city. Her hair was jet black and she wore a big red flower to the side, her skin was pale like cream silk, but with heavy eye makeup and bright red lips she was entrancing. She placed a pint in front of him and he gazed at the tattoos that covered her arms and fingers.

"Seven pounds." she demanded. Nick's mouth fell open.

"Are you kidding, seven pounds for a beer?"

"For city boys, yeah, you don't like it, go find another pub." There was a ripple of laugher from the locals and Nick begrudging handed over the note, guessing that there probably wasn't another pub round here for miles. The woman opened the till and put the money inside, not handing him over any change from the ten pound note he had just handed her. "Come on then," she ushered before he had even taken a sip. "I don't have all day to sit around waiting for you!" And with that she walked around from behind the bar, took Nick's pint and handed it to an old bloke seated next to the fire. He nodded appreciatively, then she moved over to the front door, holding it open and raising her eyebrows at Nick, suggesting he get a move on. He slid off his stool, stunned by her rudeness, but still thanked her as he went outside.

"Keys!" she commanded

Nick blinked in disbelief. "I'm not giving you my car keys!"

"Well, I'm not getting in a car with a complete stranger unless I drive! Your decision!" She folded her arms across her chest and stood defiantly. Oh God, he was tired and he just wanted to get there and shower off the dried grass goo that covered his arm. Reluctantly he threw the keys at her, and she grinned triumphantly.

"So, you're the writer are you?" she asked as she pulled away from the pub, he looked at her dubiously.

"Now how the hell would you know that?"

"Are you kidding? Did you see how big this place is when you drove in? The owner of an empty cottage calls, says he's renting out to a writer, then you walk in the pub looking like that!" She turned to look him up and down disapprovingly. "It doesn't take a genius. Everyone knows everyone's business round here," she explained. "I'm Mel, by the way," she added, softening her tone.

"Nick," he replied not happy at all, so much for anonymity. Mel smiled; she really was quite fetching, her blood-red lips drawing his attention from everything else.

"Right, here we are," she announced as she pulled up outside a modern looking cottage, unlike the others in the village the walls were a grey stone and looked like converted stables.

"Thanks, do I need to give you a lift back?" he offered, but Mel just shook her head.

"S'OK, I'll go visiting while I'm down this way." She handed over the keys and opened her door.

"Won't you get into trouble at work for just leaving and not going back?" Nick asked curiously, her puzzled look prompted him to add "...at the pub?"

"Work!" She laughed out loud. "I don't work there," she mocked, then she turned and walked down the street, her tiny rucksack balanced between her shoulder blades, her black boots kicking up dust off the road. Nick couldn't help but stare, watching her all the way up the road until she disappeared over a ridge. Who was she? Surely she was not a local and why did she serve him at the pub if she didn't work there? Weird! Resigned to accept that this was a completely different world to the one he was used to, he collected his bags and went inside.

Chapter 5

NICK COULD UNDERSTAND what George had meant when he said he had only lasted a few hours before leaving. He had arrived on Saturday and it was now only Monday morning, but already he was seriously thinking of packing up. Solitude was not all it was cracked up to be. Pine Tree Cottage was indeed beautiful, it had bright white walls with oak wood flooring, the staircase was open, with varnished wood. Modern furniture contrasted with the natural atmosphere perfectly, George obviously had a decorator come up here to renovate before he had spent his two hours in the village. The best part of the whole cottage was the main bedroom, there was a small spare room off to the side but the main bedroom was just heaven on earth. The décor was very cottage-like with flowery bedding on a four poster bed, oak beams were exposed along the ceiling and the walls, and a large stable door closed him inside. The most surprising feature was a huge cast-iron bath that was just to the side of the bed, it had obviously been a small bathroom that George had just knocked through so that the bedroom and bathroom were one. A small sink and toilet hid behind a partition giving privacy, but lying in the bath in the huge bedroom on that first night had been delightful. However, now it was Monday, the novelty had worn off and he was bored with nothing to do.

He could not focus on writing and although he had brought food for a few days he was now running out and so really needed to go shopping, and that meant venturing out into the ever nosey village, hence his dilemma as to whether to actually stay longer or not. He was not ready to return to the madness of his new celebrity life, so made the tough decision to try and stay a little longer.

He collected his wallet, first checking that he had some cash, (he doubted that the local shop took cards) and headed out. Before he had even reached his car he had been accosted by hikers who were obviously staying in the other cottages around him.

"Morning. Beautiful day, eh!" they cheerily greeted him.

"Yes it is," Nick answered politely, desperate to get away, the two hikers did not seem to be in a rush, with their waterproof coats and their long socks and trousers tucked into their boots they stood gazing around.

"You local?" the hiker continued.

"Nope just visiting." Nick now made a move to get into his car to escape, hoping they would take the hint... they didn't.

"You ever want to come out with us, just shout, there are some excellent walks round here, off the beaten track so to speak!" The hiker tapped the side of his nose as though hiding some great secret.

"Great, thanks might do that," Nick lied, and closed his car door starting the engine, the hikers bid him a 'cheerio' and set off again, walking sticks in hand. "Whoever said the country was quiet?" Nick grumbled out loud to himself as he drove up the hill towards the main street, where he was sure the Mel girl had pointed out a shop.

"Hello," Nick offered as he entered the shop, only to stop in his tracks as he saw Mel behind the counter.

"Stocking up?" she asked, as she saw the horror reflected on his face.

"Erm yeah, need to eat," he attempted to joke, she smiled.

"Whatcha need?" She paused, waiting for his response. Nick looked blank, he hadn't really thought about it, he had just intended to browse and pick up what he fancied but that was not possible in here. The counter ran like a 'U' shape all around the shop, behind it were tall shelves housing all the food and tins that they sold. On top of the counter were all the loose produce, fruit, sweets, eggs. Nick swallowed loudly whilst Mel folded her arms again.

"Why don't you tell me what you want to do and then I can help," Mel offered, her scowl slowly changing into a gentle smile. He explained that he needed lunch and tea but then he had stopped at that because that's all he needed, he wasn't sure that he even intended staying that long. Mel laughed and then began to reel off a list of things he could purchase, adding fresh bread and cheese for lunch, then offering ingredients for a chicken dinner.

She handed him a bottle of red wine to look at; he nodded, maybe a bottle of wine was just what he needed to relax. She rang all the items up and gave him the total.

"Jesus, is that the city boy price or the local price?" he spat out incredulously.

Mel cocked her head to the side. "You know this is kinda of more of a top up shop, I know we are in the back of beyond, but supermarkets do deliver, you know!" she whispered.

Nick looked at her feeling stupid, he was not in the middle of nowhere, there was probably a big store not half an hour away, it was just once you were inside the village it felt like you were trapped, well, not trapped so much as isolated. The village was like a little world in itself, the city and beyond just didn't feature in the village, it was self-sufficient and didn't need it. "So you work here then?" he asked, changing the subject to save face.

"Nope," Mel answered nonchalantly but offered no more, a long pause followed where neither one said anything. Nick awaited a response; Mel was unwilling to give one. Breaking the awkward silence, Nick paid and thanked her for her help then headed

back off to Pine Tree Cottage.
Country folk are just plain weird, he thought to himself.

Nick had just finished his lunch and was debating whether to try a bit of writing when there was a knock at the door; wondering who the hell it could be, he answered the door grumpily.

"Hi, Nick, sorry we missed you the other day, busy, busy and all that." Two people merrily chatted away. "I'm Julian," the man offered "...and this is my wife Nell." Nick smiled politely and enquired, "I'm sorry, should I know you?"

"We have been looking after the cottage for your uncle, he called to say you were coming," they explained.

"Oh right, of course, I'm sorry, please come in," Nick offered feeling rude that he had no idea who these people were, but feeling obliged to offer them a drink as they had evidently cleaned up and got the cottage ready for him. George had mentioned something about people popping in but had not given any names, and so Nick had completely forgotten about it. Julian must have been six or seven feet tall and had to duck to get through the small entrance. Nell in comparison was a tiny woman, barely reaching Julian's chest, but for some reason she also ducked when walking through the small doorway.

Nick offered them a glass of wine and settled down on the big squashy sofa in the lounge. Julian and Nell, it transpired, ran the local pub where he had stopped for directions; they were not locals as such but had been there for years. The village, though, had never really accepted them, considering them as outsiders, hence the reason for the traditional interior, an attempt to keep the locals happy and going there to drink. Not that there was anywhere else to go, but if the locals got their backs up then they could make life very difficult.

"We have run restaurants and had a wine bar at one point, that's where I met George," Nell told him. "But we just wanted to get out to the country, fresh air and tranquillity."

"We've travelled around a lot and seen so many countries but it is just so beautiful here," Nell explained. "We both came here for a visit and just fell in love with it."

Nick had to agree with them it was so beautiful around here, the colours were so vibrant and pretty. It was like someone had turned up the colour on a TV set, it was all so much brighter and clearer. He liked Julian and Nell a lot, they were so funny and had so many tales of places they had visited and people they had met, it was nice to have company. Nick was not surprised that Uncle George had kept in touch with them when they moved here, they must have been the reason George bought a cottage here in the first place.

"Listen, why don't you call into the pub tonight? Mondays are always pretty quiet and we can introduce you to the locals and make a night of it. What do you say?" Nell pleaded. "Like a 'welcome to the village' party."

Nick pulled a face. "Social functions are not really my thing," he confessed, "But thank you."

"Poppycock," Julian roared, "If you lived with old George there's no way you did not attend social functions, no excuses, Nick."

Nick smiled, he was right, life with George was one long social function, he conceded and agreed to go. Nell squealed in delight. "Can I ask?" Nick began. "When I came into the pub the other day a girl called Mel served me, but then said she didn't work there."

"Ah," Julian responded knowingly. "Yes, Mel is a bit of a free spirit around here, she doesn't really work anywhere, just helps out when people need it. She works for food, clothes, bed and board, I hardly ever pay her in cash, she just works for what she needs." Julian smiled at Nick's face, noting how intently he was listening. "Look, she will be in tonight, why don't you get to know her better?"

"Oh no, really, I was just... well interested, that's all," Nick stammered, sitting back in his seat, not realising that as Julian spoke he had leant far forward. Nell smiled broadly.

"She's a lovely girl, can't say a bad word against her, you know. Tell you what, Nick, she would be an excellent character for one of your books. Maybe you should just talk to her, get a sense of who she is, purely in a research capacity." Julian looked at his wife, knowing exactly what she was playing at.

"Yes," Nick pondered, "Maybe, yes that would be an idea, purely in the interest of research," he added. Julian and Nell just grinned at each other.

After Julian and Nell had left, Nick began to have doubts, he really didn't like parties, but then this was just a drink in the pub. He also hated being the centre of attention, that's what he was trying to get away from, but then Nell had said the pub would be quiet on a Monday night. The inner turmoil went on for a while, even as Nick lay soaking in his luxurious bath his head spun, deciding what to do. They had said that Mel would be there, but why would that influence him? Yes it was true she was very striking, individual and beautiful, she had a strong personality and took no nonsense, he had gathered that about her from just the few meetings they had had already. He wondered what her boyfriend would be like, then was horrified as he suddenly developed a sense of jealousy. What the hell was going on? He had only seen her twice, not even got to know her, he was here to escape and relax, not get involved in a relationship. He sat up in the bath suddenly, causing water to slosh over the side.

"What am I doing?" he declared out loud. "Relationship? Where the hell did that line of

thinking come from?" He blamed
Nell, she had got his author brain into gear, that's
what it was, he wasn't thinking about himself, he
was thinking about a storyline.

Drying himself off, he flicked through the
wardrobe of clothes he had brought with him; he
hadn't really packed for going out wear. All he had
brought with him was jumpers, jeans and a few
shirts. "Oh well it's only the local pub," he sighed,
and selected a reasonably smart jumper. After all he
wasn't going looking for a date, he was simply going
to research people for a story. Just to meet them, get
a sense of who they were. Where they came from.
What they liked. *Purely research*, he told himself
over and over again. But as he walked to the pub his
stomach turned over and over, this did not feel like
just research.

"Nick!" Nell called out as he entered the pub, and
she pushed her way through the crowd to get to
him.

"I thought you said Mondays were quiet!" he said,
mortified that every inch of the pub was packed
with people.

"I know, word got out, I'm sorry. People are
curious," she said, completely unapologetic.

Nick sighed a long painful sigh; this was going to
be a long night, he thought, as he took a long breath
on his inhaler. He stood trying to decide whether to

make a run for it when a young girl sauntered up to him

"Mr Mill-Thorpe, I read your book and I have to say I loved it," she gushed "It so exciting to have a proper famous person here." Nick pasted on his work smile and nodded gratefully, trying to step around her but she blocked his path and continued, "I mean when I heard you were coming, I just thought, like, God, I so have to meet you, it's like destiny or something." Nick cringed; he needed to have Melissa here to help him deal with situations like this, what was he supposed to do?

"Put your claws back in, Tracy!" a voice called out, causing the young girl to practically hiss.

"Piss off reject, I'm talking to Nick!" She returned her gaze to him, smiling sickly. Nick's instincts went on red alert as the girl practically pointed her cleavage in his direction. But he hardly noticed as he strained around the girl to see who was defending him, only to come face to face with her, the Goth girl, Mel. Words failed him; Mel's hair was now a bright orange, her black vest allowed her tattooed arms to be on display.

"Talking? What a joke! Talk with your chest, do you?" Mel leaned over into Tracy's cleavage "...and tell me, Tracy's tits, what valuable information have you learned from our local celebrity?" Nick suppressed a chuckle as Tracy's face practically turned purple, but Mel did not allow her to get another word in. "Listen, Tracy! Get lost, go point

your tits in someone else's face and
shut your gob or I will shut it for ya," she continued.
Tracy gave her a filthy look that on anyone else
would have probably intimidated them, but Mel was
different, she just smiled a sarcastic smile and led
Nick away by the arm.

"I don't know how to thank you, I get this all the
time it's so unnerving," he began.

"Don't flatter yourself." Mel brushed off his
comment. "Tracy will sink her claws into anyone
that she thinks might get her out of here." She
moved behind the bar to get them some drinks
"Beer?"

"Wine please, red," Nick murmured, stunned by
her harshness, Julian caught a glimpse of him and
waved, Nick nodded in return.

"So you have always lived here? You never
fancied leaving?" Nick asked. "Going into the city one
day?" Mel just laughed.

"Lived here all my life and have you seen it round
here, why would anyone want to leave?" Her
honesty showed, and Nick could see that she truly
believed that, Mel had no intentions of going
anywhere. She intrigued him, he was desperate to
know more, question her, find out every little piece
of information he could.

She placed a bottle of wine in front of him. "Julian
says you might need the bottle!" she joked, and

Julian could be seen giggling in the background. As he took a sip, someone else came to talk to him and began to ask him about his writing, it was weird, he usually hated all this attention but these people were genuinely interested in him, his story. Mel sat next to him and listened as he talked, unbeknownst to him quietly topping up his glass as soon as it emptied, a curious expression on her face.

Chapter 6

NICK'S HEAD SPUN, he didn't want to open his eyes as he knew the light would stab through his tender eyeballs, causing him searing pain. Then there was this heavy weight on his chest, like someone or something was sitting on him. He didn't even remember getting home last night, he remembered talking, a lot, he had been really happy. Mel had been refilling his glass and he had drunk, he couldn't begin to think how much he had drunk. Daring to be brave, he slowly opened his eyes, allowing the light to flood his brain, and he struggled to focus. Slowly but surely his eyes adjusted and he came face to face with a white Jack Russell sitting squarely in the middle of his chest, as his brain began to digest this unusual information he let out a girly shriek as his eyes spotted a dead rat at the dog's feet.

"What the..? Get it off me!" he cried out.

"Oh for goodness sake, Fatso, was there any need for that?" Mel walked across to the bed, picked up the dead rat by the tail and slung it out of the window. "I will deal with that later."

Oh God, what had he done! He looked around him and the realisation dawned upon him that he was not in his own bed. Mel grinned at him as he lifted the sheet up to see if he was dressed underneath. "Don't worry, I didn't attack you or anything," she smirked. "You lost your keys, probably at the pub, I couldn't be bothered going back so you stayed here for the night." Nick let out a sigh of relief and cradled his head. "Here, have a coffee," she offered handing him a mug. Mel stood unashamedly in her vest and underwear, banging mugs together as she made another coffee for herself. Nick swallowed hard, trying not to stare.

"Who are your friends?" he asked, pointing at the three pups who sat at her feet.

"They work on the farm, just come to visit, don't you, boys?" She affectionately scratched the ear of the smallest dog. "I suppose you want a reward for that capture, do you?" she asked the dogs, all three now sat bolt upright, straight as statues puffing out their snow white chests. "They catch rats, stops 'em eating the grain. You wouldn't believe the damage those tiny things can do," she explained, whilst cutting up three small pieces of cheese. "This one is Fatso," she introduced, handing over the piece of cheese that the pup gobbled down so quickly it probably didn't even touch the sides of his mouth, let alone have time to allow the dog to taste it. "He never let any of the others feed, he was so greedy when he was born and ended up a fat little round pup. This one is Billy." Billy's ears pricked up at the sound of his name, and his little stub of a tail wagged rapidly, expecting his treat. "...And this little boy is Toby, he was the runt but he can't half stand up for himself now." She tickled the little one's ears and his head tilted appreciatively. "Go on now, skedaddle," she shooed the dogs out through the little cat flap on her door. "Their mother is heavily pregnant at the moment so they are being naughty, taking advantage of the fact she can't keep up with them," she laughed.

"You like animals then?" Nick asked, pulling the cover up to hide his embarrassment of discovering himself in a stranger's bed, and taking a sip of the life-saving black liquid in his mug.

"Why wouldn't I?" she asked, puzzled, grabbing her coffee and sliding into the bed next to him. "Don't worry," she teased, noting how he flinched as she climbed in, "You're not that cute, I think you're safe!"

"Sorry," Nick began. "I just... we're not usually this friendly with people we don't know."

"Well it's MY bed so really it's YOU that's being inappropriate, not me." She rolled her eyes, bored with conversation.

"So this is your place?" Nick asked, trying to change the conversation

"Yeah, well it's one of many." She told him that she spent most of her time there, her dad converted the space over one of his barns when she had hit eighteen, he thought she needed some space to put down some roots, she laughed ironically at her own words. The room was tiny, there was her bed, a small square table with one chair and a kitchen unit with a sink, he presumed there must have been a little bathroom somewhere but that was it, very basic, very small. He looked down at the cover on the bed, it was an intricate patchwork quilt, each patch had something different stitched onto it, a tree, an animal, a slogan, his mother would love something like this.

Mel watched him stroking each patch, she really didn't understand him, most of the guys her age that came through the village were either adrenaline junkies looking for extreme sport locations or guys returning to visit families. Nick wasn't like any of them, he was shy and nervous, putting his foot in his mouth at every opportunity, but after a few drinks he had changed. Talking about his book and his ideas, he had spoken so passionately, so animated about his projects, it was fascinating to listen to him. As his words had become more and more slurred Mel had hidden his house keys, curious to see what he would do, curious to see if he would turn into one of the stereotypical guys she knew but no, he had offered to sleep on the floor. Even drunk, he had been the perfect gentleman, much to Mel's surprise and, she had to admit, slight disappointment.

"Where would you buy something like this?" he asked, wrenching her from her thoughts, "My mum would love this."

Mel smiled. "My dad made it for me, each patch represents something I like or a point in my life." She pointed to a small white square, "This is my baby blanket." She pointed to another, "this was my favourite t-shirt when I was five." She went on to tell him about each square, each patch representative of a happy memory. Her whole life was laid out in front of him in squares. Her first school uniform, a patch from her first riding jumper, her first boiler suit. All her hobbies and things she loved were delicately sewn together for him to see.

"It's amazing," Nick said, completely in awe "He must be a lovely guy, your dad, building skills and sewing skills, amazing"

Mel pursed her lips. "Same title different men." She raised her eyebrows. "I have two dads, well a few really but two mainly." Nick blinked slowly, his head thumped and he wasn't sure his brain was making any sense of what she was saying. "Look, don't worry about it, my life; com-pli-cated!" She had no idea why she was explaining herself to him, he had no idea how weird and unconventional her life was, no one did, but she never felt the need to explain herself to anyone, it was none of their business.

After a long pause Nick approached the topic of the previous night. "Did I make a fool of myself?" he asked sheepishly. "I don't usually drink that much, my uncle says I'm a lightweight," he admitted, feeling ashamed and hoping that he hadn't been an idiot.

"No, nothing like that," Mel reassured him. "You are as charming drunk as you are sober."

"Really?" Nick grinned ear to ear. "So you think I'm charming?" Somehow learning this had made Nick forget about his hangover, and his heart had flipped a somersault. Mel cursed herself for her slip up, yes, he was charming, he was very appealing and she had felt a pull to him that she had never felt before, but she did not do relationships and this young pup had no chance.

"I need to get ready," Mel announced, stepping out of bed, "Help yourself to whatever you want, just shut the door when you leave." She walked around a corner and Nick heard water running, *that must be the bathroom*, he guessed. Hugging his cup, he snuggled down into the bed again, stunned at what had happened. He had got drunk and slept in Mel's bed, next to her, and didn't remember a thing but this morning, yes this morning he had felt her, felt her bare thigh brush against his as she voluntarily climbed into bed next to him. He was in trouble he knew it, he knew it the minute he had seen her in the pub, the minute her flash of orange hair had saved him from the clutches of a local gold-digger.

This tiny little place where she lived didn't even have a cooker, didn't even look lived in. A million questions swirled around his already spinning head; who was she and why did she have multiple parents and multiple homes? She didn't look like she fitted in with the village in any way, but spending time with her proved that she was a part of the village, it was her home, she was a conundrum that he wanted to solve. He took a quick a peek at his watch and swore loudly.

"It's half past six!" he raged. "Half past six in the morning, what the hell!" Mel came out of the bathroom, her toothbrush hanging out of her mouth

"I know, I slept in a bit, Joe and Freddy will go mad, I'm supposed to be helping out on the farm today!" and she sauntered back into the bathroom grabbing some clothes and a make-up bag.

"Half past six," Nick repeated, dumbstruck, "Who the hell gets up at half past six?" He was contemplating pulling the covers up and returning to sleep when a thought struck him, he had no idea where he was, no idea how to get back to his cottage. Slowly he pulled the covers back and pulled on his jeans quickly before Mel remerged from the bathroom, God, it was cold at this time in the morning. It was the height of summer, yet at half past six the floor was freezing on his bare feet, and his toes curled in retaliation.

"Any chance you can point me in the right direction so that I can get home?" he asked hopefully. Mel appeared from the bathroom and again he caught his breath, even in a green boiler suit she was gorgeous. She had a tight, white vest on, allowing the top of the suit to hang by her waist, her orange hair was swept up into a loose knot on the top of her head, a cream, flowery scarf wrapped around forming a hairband, but her trademark dark eyes and ruby lips were firmly in place.

"Sure," she replied nonchalantly, then smiled a shy smile as she realised he was standing staring at her with his mouth hanging open!

She slammed the door shut and gingerly headed down the rickety narrow steps, Nick following close behind. She waved over to two huge men who were standing beside a quad bike, drinking from mugs that were steaming through the early morning fresh air. Nick shrunk back as they moved towards them both.

"I'm just gonna point Nick in the right direction to get home then I will be back, OK?" she shouted over to them. The two large men looked Nick up and down.

"So you're Nick-ol-arse, are you?" one of the men asked sarcastically, causing the other one to chortle out loud.

"Freddy, be nice!" Mel warned, waving a finger in his face. Nick grimaced, the guys must have been over six feet tall and both built like brick houses. These must be the two brothers that Mel called her dads, Nick shuddered to think which one had done the intricate stitching on the quilt and was certainly not about to ask. He nodded his head in a greeting and ushered Mel to move further up the road.

"Ignore them, they're all bark and no bite," she said confidently.

"That remains to be seen," Nick muttered. Mel pointed the way back to the village, he couldn't get lost, it was just a straight road to the pub; he would have to go there first to pick up his keys that were probably behind the bar. Julian and Nell were early risers, Mel assured him, so they would be up to open for him. Then he could head home and return to bed, sleep off his headache. How Mel was going to manage working on the farm was beyond him, either she had guts of steel or she hadn't drunk as much as him. "Never again," he muttered to himself as he staggered up the road towards the pub again.

Chapter 7

NICK SIPPED HIS coffee and opened the doors to the little garden that lay at the back of Pine Tree Cottage. His head had now just about returned to normal after his exploits at the pub, and then finding himself in a strange woman's bed with no idea where he was. He had sunk straight back into bed as soon as he returned home and had slept most of the day, desperate to relieve his throbbing headache. But today, this morning, he felt OK and now he sat in an exquisite small garden, reflecting about the past two days. The sun shone brightly, warming his face, and Nick found himself closing his eyes, basking in its glory, warming his very soul. At first he had found the village dull, the pace of life was frantic for the villagers but for visitors it was quiet and peaceful. He had found it excruciating to begin with, today though, he had no need to rush, no need to be somewhere important or talk to anyone, today he could just be.

The garden had a small patio area set out with table and chairs just by the windows, there was a small patch of grass with beautiful wild flowers growing in and around it. Nick wondered if George paid someone to maintain the garden, keeping it so charming. A low stone wall encircled the property, allowing him to view out of the garden and beyond. He could see over the rolling hills and dales where its varied coloured fields were spotted with sheep and cattle. At the same time, high bushes to the side gave him privacy from the cottages and farms around him, forcing his view forward into the countryside.

A strange noise forced him to open his eyes, and adjusting to the bright sunlight he saw a beautiful, majestic fox returning his stare. It was sleek and shining in the sun, its white paws gingerly testing the ground before placing each footstep. Nick found himself holding his breath; he had never been so close to such a beautiful, wild creature. Not daring to move, he remained frozen in his seat as the fox slowly moved to the right, ascertaining that he was no threat it began sniffing the ground, always keeping one eye on Nick. A smile slowly spread across his face, it was a magical, precious moment that he could never…

"Go on. Get!" a voice yelled out, and a gunshot rang through Nick's ears.

"No!" he called out, desperately running over to the fox to see if it had been hit; the fox, however, was long gone, certainly not hanging around now. An angry man in a brown jacket ran towards Nick.

"What the hell are you doing? You don't encourage them creatures around here, idiot!" he bellowed. Nick remained stunned.

"You were going to shoot it," he whispered almost to himself.

"Too bloody right, I got my chickens just over there, that beast in't getting anywhere near here!" Nick gathered himself together.

"You listen to me, this is my property and you have no right to SHOOT into my land, you ever do that again and I will call the authorities, you...you monster!" he screamed. The man didn't so much as flinch, he simply snarled and walked away muttering, "Bloody townies, no idea."

Nick was now trembling in anger; he never lost his temper but that man had tried to hurt that creature, that beautiful, enchanting creature. *Country folk have no emotional attachment to animals*, Nick thought. That wild animal had just wandered into his garden, they had shared a connection, stared into each other's eyes; it had been the single most amazing experience of his life. Nick tried to clear his mind of the surreal meeting, tried to force himself to sit down and disappear into his writing, but every time he did all he could think about was those deep penetrating eyes of the fox. Surrendering to the notion that concentration was impossible, he decided to go for a walk, maybe he could visit the little cafe or just have a mooch around to see what was what. He tried to resist the fluttering in his heart when he thought of the idea that he might bump into Mel again.

The cafe was at the very top of the village, it was a steep climb, and by the time Nick had reached it he was out of breath and in need of more than coffee.

His legs shook, and he thought that if he didn't sit down soon he might just fall down. How did he get this much out of shape? He worked out in the gym, he swam regularly but then he hadn't done much of anything lately, wow, it was worrying how quickly his body had suffered due to his busy schedule. His asthma had decreased in its severity the older he got, but he still felt the need to keep his inhaler close, if not just for times like this. As he puffed through the door, a shaky voice laughed at him,

"Good grief, lad, come and sit down you look positively done in!"

An old lady took his hand and sat him in the first seat she could find. She had a kind face, and snow white hair cascaded around her face. "I'm Rose," she introduced herself. "I run this cafe with my sister, Alice." Nick managed a smile after he had taken two long puffs of his inhaler, and eventually he began to regain his composure.

"I'm so sorry, that hill is just a killer, I don't know how you manage it," Nick gasped, his wheezing reducing gradually to a normal quiet breath.

"Practice," Rose giggled, she had an addictive, girly laugh and Nick couldn't help but like her, she had a naughty little twinkle in her eyes that told him she had an interesting past. His perpetually curious author brain kicked in, and he silently began concocting a background story for her. "So you're the author in town?" she asked, settling herself

down next to him; before he could
reply a crass voice called out from the kitchen.

"Rose! Rose, stop gassing to the customers and
try taking an order for once." Rose just rolled her
eyes. "She really is a delight to work with, you
know," she said sarcastically. "She is right though,
what can we offer you?"

"Erm, I was coming for a coffee but I think I need
a cold drink now!" He suddenly became aware of the
sweat that was trickling down his neck. Rose gave
him a knowledgeable nod.

"I think tea is in order, good for rehydration." She
leaned in. "Why don't you go take a seat out the back
and I will bring it out to you."

Reluctantly Nick attempted to stand, thank
goodness his legs had regained some of their
strength and he was able to slowly move out to the
back of the café. The sight that greeted him took his
breath away. From this height if he looked left, he
could see the entire village, small houses dotted the
scenery, farms with tiny figures moving around. To
the right his view stretched for miles, miles and
miles of Mother Nature. There was not a house or
building in sight, just luscious greenery with all
range of textures and terrain. Was there not one bit
of flat land around here?

"Here you go, love, you sit yourself down." Rose
appeared with an ornate china teapot, a teacup and
saucer and a plate of biscuits, all displayed with

great finesse on a silver tray. On the side was a glass of iced water.

"That's perfect," Nick sighed appreciatively, guessing he wasn't the first person to be caught out by the treacherous hill. Rose placed the tray on the table and turned to leave. "Please join me," Nick invited, "If you're not busy of course".

"Dear, you are my only customer," she beamed delightedly. Another lady that Nick presumed to be the sister Alice came out from the café.

"I'm off to do the veggie plot, do you think you can manage?" she asked Rose, who just smiled at her sweetly. "You're not gonna hear customers come in if you are out here!"

"For goodness sake, Alice, there's a bell on the door, I will hear anyone that comes in!" she complained. Alice let out a sigh and strutted around the corner of the café. "Ignore her," Rose offered, "She was never the same after Bill left her, ran off with a younger woman, been bitter ever since. We opened the café just after, I had hoped it might cheer her up a bit but... well you can see the results," she chuckled, rolling her eyes once more. Nick laughed.

"And what about you, Rose? No man in your life?" Nick regretted his question immediately, as Rose's smile slipped. "I'm sorry, it's none of my business." Rose's smile fixed back into place.

"Don't be silly, dear; it's your nature to be curious. We used to laugh, you know, my husband was called William also, Bill and Bill." She stared off into the distance. "It's silly, really, he got a cold, just a simple cold. It developed into flu, then pneumonia, then one day he just didn't wake up." Nick's eyes welled with tears as he saw all the pain and remorse in this wonderful old woman's face. "I'm so sorry."

"It was a long time ago, he was a lovely man. Not unlike your uncle." She steered the conversation away from the painful memories of her beloved Bill. "You know, he hated the village the moment he set foot in it." This was not news to Nick; Uncle George had told him how bored he was. "It's funny really, because we all liked him straight away, he made such an impression."

"Yeah," Nick agreed. "George tends to do that a lot."

"I will not have a bad word spoken about your uncle, lad, I found him to be an honest and respectable man." Nick snorted his water out, 'respectable' was not a word often used in the same sentence as his Uncle George. George, who had given Nick his cigar to try at the age of just ten!

Nick had been correct, as they sat and drank their delicious tea Rose regaled him with tales of village life, all the people that had come and gone. She delighted in telling him that at seventy-two years old she still managed to run a business and maintain her own garden, as well as be an active member of the village community group. It also appeared that she was the one who had kept Pine Tree Cottage's garden so beautiful and in keeping with the cottage's style. The bell interrupted their conversation.

"It's only me, Rose," a familiar voice called out.

"We are out back, love," Rose called back and as Nick had expected, Mel walked through the doors. Her hair was back to jet black and she wore it up loosely tied up in a red patterned scarf. Nick's heart began to pulse and his hands knotted together, that simple act did not go unnoticed by Rose.

"Oh, you again," Mel muttered, but her eyes smiled. "I can't seem to get away from you these days."

"Well that's what happens when you invite a man into your bed," Rose reprimanded. Nick's eyes widened in shock and embarrassment.

"Nothing happened, Rose!" Mel defended. "Where else was he gonna go?"

"Where indeed?" Rose smiled coyly, enjoying the intense atmosphere that was now developing, not to mention Nick's now beetroot-red face.

"Did you want me for something?" Mel shook her head, giving in and choosing not to argue with the old woman. Rose was sharp as a tack, she could

wheedle information out of anyone
before they even realised they had confessed a
word.

Rose needed some cash taking down to Mr
Michaels who ran the local shop that Nick had seen
Mel working in. Rose had borrowed change from the
man on Monday and needed to return it now that
her sister had cashed up at the bank. It was a
frequent arrangement between the two businesses,
as the bank was a good hour's drive away.

"Why don't you keep Mel company, Nick?" Rose
suggested mischievously. Mel shot her a disgusted
look. "I would feel better, dear, there is over two
hundred pounds in change." Nick was already
standing to his feet and thanking Rose for the drink,
before Mel had chance to complain. Looking over
her shoulder as they left, Mel mouthed, "I hate you,"
to Rose, who just shrugged her shoulders and blew
her a kiss.

Going downhill somehow seemed worse than
going up, Nick's calves strained as he struggled to
keep his balance. He told Mel all about the events of
the morning and how beautiful the fox had been.
How shocked he had been when the farmer had
heartlessly pulled a gun on the beautiful animal;
Mel, however, rolled her eyes at him, a habit that
was starting to get on his nerves, making him feel
like a little kid.

"You don't understand the damage these animals
do, Nick, it's not that we don't care about animals,

it's because we care about our own animals," she tried to explain. Nick couldn't understand why anyone would want to deliberately hurt a beautiful wild animal, so they were forced to agree to disagree. As they walked rain appeared from nowhere, there was not a cloud in the sky but still there was a fine spray of water in the air, thicker than mist but not quite rain. Mel seemed unperturbed by this and carried on carelessly, chatting away to him about her dad's farm.

"Oh my God, look at that!" Nick broadcast excitedly, stopping suddenly in his tracks and gazing over the wall to his right. Right before his eyes an elaborate rainbow had appeared, arcing over the fields. "It's a full arch," he gasped, "I have never seen a full arch before, look you can see exactly where it begins and where it ends, isn't it amazing?" He stood transfixed like an excited child, the vibrant colours leapt out from the picture perfect background that spread out behind it. He had seen pale rainbows before but this one looked like it had been freshly painted in the sky, and never had he seen a full rainbow.

"That's what happens where there are no buildings or factories in the way to block it" As Mel admired his view her hand reached down and grasped his tightly, he tore himself away from the rainbow to check that what he felt was actually happening. The warmth of her skin pressing against his, the sudden jolt he felt as her fingers brushed his. He slowly raised his gaze, looking deep into her eyes and smiled; it was as though time stood still, the rain soaking them gently and slowly without either one noticing or caring. No words were needed, as they turned once more to look at the rainbow that now practically shone as the colours became brighter and brighter the more Nick stared, his heart overflowing with joy. "Come on," Mel shoved his shoulder, nudging him to move but he refused to let go of her hand and began dragging her with him.

After dropping the money off with Mr Michaels, Nick asked Mel if she fancied keeping him company for a bit. "Sure, I think I can spare you an hour or two," she agreed.

"Oh well, don't force yourself will you!" he joked, still keeping a tight grip on her hand as they walked towards Pine Tree Cottage. Never had he felt like this, his heart was swelling every time he was with her, and now holding hands walking together just felt so right.

"Hey, what's that?" Mel asked as she heard a voice coming from the back of the cottage. Nick walked around the side of the house, then came to a sudden stop and gasped in horror at the sight that greeted him. There were feathers all over his beautiful garden, dead chickens strewn around, blood everywhere. Mel pushed passed him to see if any were alive, the angry man was leaning against the wall staring at the horrific sight, the look he gave Nick said all he needed to say. Mel turned to him sympathetically

"It's not your fault, Nick," she reassured.

"Sure, it's never the townies' fault, is it!" the man bellowed. "Do you see? Do you see why we don't let them around here? It hasn't even eaten them; it's just killed them, all of them. Take a good look at your garden, Nick!" He kicked a carcass out of his way; Nick was forced to side step to avoid it hitting him. "This is what happens when you don't respect our ways!" he scolded, then stomped off back to his farm.

"Come on, I'll help you clean up," Mel offered but Nick was mortified, could not move. That beautiful creature, it had just killed, not one chicken had been eaten, it had just ripped every single one into pieces. The luscious green grass was now striped with blood red lines, body parts of the chickens scattered the once beautiful haven, and it was all his fault. "I'm so sorry," Mel tried to comfort him but Nick was inconsolable. "I'd better go and help see if he needs help fixing the chicken coop," she told him, squeezing his hand gently and standing up onto her tiptoes to kiss him on the cheek. Gathering himself together, he retrieved a black bin bag from the kitchen, and using gardening gloves began the arduous task of cleaning up the brutal slaughter.

Chapter 8

NICK NO LONGER saw the majestic fox when he closed his eyes, all he saw were the bloody corpses of chickens, ripped and torn apart. He had been stupid and naive to think that country life was something he could adapt to, he was a city boy, always would be. The night offered no relief for Nick, he tried to sleep but his thoughts were filled with the farmer's eyes, the disgust he obviously felt for Nick more than apparent. Perhaps he should offer compensation for the loss of his animals, but there was more than regret over financial loss in that man's eyes, there was pain.

Nick contemplated packing up and leaving, just going home, leaving all this behind him and returning to where he belonged. As he was about to start packing there was a knock at the door, he left it, feeling unable to face anyone, but the person knocking was relentless and the banging just got louder and louder.   Throwing the door open annoyed, he came face to face with Mel.

"Hey, thought you might fancy some company today," she smiled and held up a picnic basket. "I know this wonderful spot that will make you forget all your troubles." Nick looked rough, no sleep had left him with dark circles round his eyes, he still had the same clothes on that he had worn the day before that were now all rumpled.

"I'm grateful, Mel, but I really am not in the mood," he said sadly. Mel just put her hands on her hips.

"I'm sorry, did I give you the impression that you had a choice? I'm sorry, let me rephrase it...get in the shower, change clothes and get your arse out of this house and on a picnic with me. I will put you in the shower myself if I have to!" The determination in her face made Nick actually laugh, Mel reminded him so much of his Uncle George.

"Do you know, I believe you would," he confirmed.

When he had showered and dressed, Mel took his hand in hers and they strolled through the village hand in hand, and Nick felt that familiar feeling of warmth spread through him as though the drama of the day before had never happened. As they walked, people offered greetings to them both, Mel seemed to know everyone.

"Mel, are you free this week I need a hand with....", "Mel, I've got that book in if you want to come around...", "Hi Mel, fancy cooking tea for my dad on Thursday, my mum is away ..."

Always they were greeted with a 'sure, no problem'. Nick watched her as she chatted away to everyone, asking how everyone was, knowing everyone's business but never gossiping about it to anyone else. She really was a well-liked member of this village.

"Is there anyone that doesn't like you around here?" he asked jokingly

"There's plenty," she assured him, "...But yeah I guess, this is my home, my village, everyone is like my family." Nick believed her completely, she had a look whenever she talked about the village or the Dales like a mother talking about her child, she always smiled and her eyes glazed over with fondness. Nick began to think that Mel could not belong anywhere else, the city would just swallow her up; here, she shone brightly.

The path that they were walking along began to dwindle and Mel easily climbed over a low stone wall. "Erm, are we allowed to do this?" Nick asked nervously, Mel just laughed.

"It's not private property, Nick, the Dales belong to everyone and everyone looks after the Dales." She took his hand again and Nick felt all his worries and concerns fade into insignificance. They were heading towards a thick wood, fully bloomed trees dominated the landscape their foliage offering relief from the now searing midday sun. Mel looked at him excitedly, now practically pulling him through the trunks that obscured their view. When she finally stopped Nick just stood aghast, just when he thought he had seen the most beautiful sights, this area just threw something more extraordinary in his face. Mel grinned as she stood before the most majestic waterfall. Lime green leaves framed the powerful white water as it hurtled down the drop, creating white waves as it hit the rocks and pond below. Just like a movie set, it was perfect down to the smooth rocks ideally arranged so that they could sit on them, this couldn't have been created more perfectly.

"What do you think?" Mel asked, a little unsure.

"I can't even find the words," Nick began. "It's just ...stunning." Mel grinned.

"Wow, if an author can't find the words it must be good." Mel had always thought the Dales were the most beautiful place on this earth but few people really saw its true beauty. They looked at the sights and walked through the pre-set paths but they didn't connect, didn't feel. The Dales were her life, every beat of her heart could be linked here, she could not imagine living anywhere else. Mel watched as Nick breathed heavily, taking in each minute detail of the waterfall, felt the spray cooling his face. He felt it, the power, the feelings it projected into your very soul, he understood.

Grabbing the basket from Mel, Nick began to spread out the blanket on the ground, suddenly ravenous. Mel had made an amazing spread, all was homemade. Sandwiches, pies and salads, there were jars of chutneys and pickles, it was staggering, this woman constantly surprised him.

"This is unbelievable," he praised "Thank you, you really are an enigma, Mel."

"Why?" she asked.

"I don't know...I mean no offence but you don't exactly fit in with the village, you know," Nick said gently, not wanting to offend or upset her but Mel just shrugged.

"I am what I am, I can't be anything else." She confided in him that her mother had died when she was young, she never knew her father and so two farmers, Joe and Freddy, had taken her in and raised her, well, all the village had raised her, really.

"They would be the delightful giants I met the other day," Nick commented.

"Yeah, I have the greatest dads in the entire world," she said proudly

"So have they ever been married?" Nick asked, Mel looked confused.

"Married? I don't think the village is quite ready for that yet." Now it was Nick's turn to feel confused.

"Eh?" Then the penny dropped. "Oh, I thought they were brothers," he confessed.

"No, what gave you that idea?" Mel asked. She explained that Joe and Freddy had grown up on neighbouring farms and had been close friends from an early age, no one questioned it but as they grew up their friendship grew also. When the families had found out how the boys really felt about each other they had disowned the boys, basically throwing them out. They had left their village with nothing but the clothes on their backs, but hard work and determination brought them to this village. The money they had saved over the years of working on various farms, moving around from village to village, bought them a farm and they were making it work, putting their families to the back of their minds and forging a future for themselves. The villagers had never given them a second thought, they were good, kind, hardworking folk and that was all that mattered.

Nick listened as Mel told him all about the farm, and how she was always into mischief growing up there. She loved the animals, being around them, she told him that she could find calmness from their peace.

"My parents also died when I was young," he began. "I had the greatest adoptive parents too, my mum struggled when Dad died but she's getting on her feet again, it's good." As they talked more and more they found they had so much in common, music, books, food it was weird, like they were two halves of the whole.

"So does this place have a name?" Nick asked, shoving the last piece of sponge cake into his mouth, his belly already too full, but he couldn't resist. The woods were called 'The Whispering Woods' so called by the kids that used to play there. On a windy day the wind would howl through the treetops, making it sound like a ghost wailing or screaming.

They used to have bets as to how long each one would last. Of course Mel would always win.

"It never scared me, the noise, I never found it haunting like the other children did, I thought it was more like ...a mother singing, I think," she explained. "It's so lovely here, how could anyone ever find it scary? Of course, its reputation also means I often have the place to myself cause everyone gets freaked out here!" she added cheekily. Then she suddenly stood up and without warning stripped down her jeans

"Erm... What are we doing?" Nick asked, nervously shifting position,

"We? I don't know what WE are doing but I am going for a swim," and with that her vest went up over her head, leaving her standing in her bra and pants. Nick inhaled sharply, he was staring, he knew he was staring but he couldn't take his eyes off her. She was like the fox in his garden, wild and unpredictable but would she cause him the same pain? Would she rip out his heart like the fox ripped out the throats of those chickens?

In one swift movement Mel dived and slipped through the water with hardly a splash into the pool, resurfacing about six feet away, nearly reaching the other side in one stroke. She turned to face him

"You coming in?" she asked

"Not on your nelly! It's freezing!" he rebuked.

"Chicken!" she called out as she disappeared again under the water. Nick watched her back under the surface as she swam towards the waterfall, parting it like a pair of curtains she disappeared behind it. It was her favourite place to relax, the thundering water blocked out the outside world and from the outside no one would be able to see her, she could vanish from the world like the characters in Nick's book. Not that she had told him that she had read it; not only had she read it, she had loved it. Night after night she had worked at the Jonson's farm, helping out so that she could read their daughters copy. His story had made her heart soar, the characters had been through so much and survived, coming out stronger than ever. Mel had thought it was the most amazing story. Taking a deep breath, she dived under once more and glided soundlessly back towards him, then hauled herself out of the pool to lay on the rock. To Nick she looked like an angel, the water on her skin glistened like delicate crystals that were embedded in a rock face. She stretched out, allowing the dappled sunlight to dry her off, Nick should have felt embarrassed watching this practically naked woman but he wasn't, he was enthralled, drinking in every little detail like a thirsty traveller.

"You have a lot of tattoos," he stated the obvious, Mel just smiled.

"Do they have meaning?" he asked, wanting to know every little thing about her. She sat forward;

"My arms," she pointed, "these are element inks, earth, wind, fire, water, they remind me that we are all susceptible to Mother Nature, something you learn very quickly when you live out here. These..." she pointed to her shoulders, "...are local butterflies, they don't live long but when they are here they are everywhere and so beautiful, but the dogs do tend to chase them all over, it's quite funny really." She turned her back to him and he found himself reaching out to touch the long design that contoured her spine. "These represent my favourite place in the world, there is a field just outside the village very, very high up. No good for grazing or anything and at a certain time of year it is covered in buttercups, the most beautiful yellow you have ever seen, it almost lights up the sky." She turned back to face him, a shy, almost embarrassed expression on her face. "I would like to take you... I mean if you come back this way next year." Nick caught his breath.

"Right now I never want to leave." He leaned in and placed his lips against hers, her lips were moist and still wet from the water, her soaking wet strands of hair falling around his face. Pulling himself away, he gently pushed the strands of hair aside curling them around her ears.

"You're not like the usual guys that pass through here," she spoke softly. "If they saw me sitting here like this they'd be on me like a rash."

"Maybe I don't want the same things those guys wanted." Nick was honest in his response, Mel lowered her head,

"What do you want? I mean, you won't stay forever and I don't do relationships very well." Her face was strained as though fighting an inner turmoil.

"I don't know what I want," he confessed. "I'm kind of winging it at the moment, when I came here I didn't count on falling....I mean liking someone whilst I was here." Nick told her about the pressure he faced as a successful author, and the girl in his hotel room that prompted him to get away.

"I have to make a confession," Mel began. "I have read your book, I read it as soon as it came out, that's kind of the reason I wanted to bring you here. You described in your book a place where the girl could hide away, a secret space behind a waterfall." Nick sat back, confounded. "I figured someone like you would appreciate this place and what it means to me." She lowered her eyes and Nick knew she was telling him things she had never told anyone before, that she was baring a little piece of her soul to him.

"Did you enjoy it?" he asked, pride flushing through him, Mel smiled.

"It's good, you are talented. I kind of got you drunk on purpose in the pub first night you were here. I'm sorry, I mean I just wanted to see if you were the guy I hoped you were, or whether you would turn out like all the others."

Nick felt himself becoming amused, Mel liked him, she had tested him. He should have been furious at her actions but instead he felt a warm relief fill his very soul.

"And?"

"You were good, you just wanted to sleep, never touched, never suggested, a perfect gent...unfortunately." Mel moved closer to him, taking his head in her hands. "I liked it," she added before pressing herself against him, her lips pressed firmly against his. Nick groaned, he had fantasised about this, dreamed about it and now here he was in the most beautiful surroundings with the most beautiful girl in his arms. 'Please let it not be a dream,' he thought. Mel's lips moved over his cheek, kissing him, caressing him, placing gentle kisses up his cheek and towards his ear. He gasped as she took his earlobe between her teeth, nibbling gently then slowly nuzzling down his neck. She placed one leg over his and climbed onto his lap, straddling him

"I think I may be starting to really like you, Nick," she whispered.

"You haven't left my thoughts since I arrived here, Mel," Nick replied lost in a sea of pleasure, he could not have written a more perfect scene.

Chapter 9

THE MEMORY OF Mel's lips replayed in Nick's head over and over again, it had taken every single ounce of restraint he had not to take things further. She was unlike any other girl he had known; she was confident but shy at times, and outrageous in her dress and style but conservative with her heart. He was falling, he knew it and if he was honest he didn't want to stop, ever. Mel made his heart skip every time he saw her, he wanted to see her all the time, call her just to hear her voice, but Mel had no phone, mobile or landline. She flitted around the village like every home was her own, every family was her family, and she was fiercely protective of her privacy. Nick could understand that, wasn't that why he was here in the village in the first place?

It was now Sunday and the wonderful picnic with Mel had been on Thursday but Nick had not seen Mel since. He had strolled into the village for no reason, hoping to casually bump into her but no. He had even bravely ventured up to the farm.

"'Ello Nick-ol-arse," Freddy had greeted him with his usual turn of phrase, emphasising the 'arse' part. Nick had tried to sound confident but guessed his voice came out shaky and childlike when he asked if Mel was around, because Freddy roared with laughter. "Mel, what on earth would Mel wanna hang out with you for, Nick-ol-arse?" Embarrassed,

Nick had turned tail and left only to have Joe, Mel's other dad, come running after him.

"Ignore him, he's playing with you," Joe comforted. "She's not here, she's staying in the village for a couple of days, there's some work to do. I don't know where but she will be staying with a couple of people over the next few days, I think." Nick's face fell, obviously the picnic hadn't left as big of an impression on Mel as it had on Nick. He thanked Joe despondently. "She likes you, you know," Joe added before he left. "She hasn't really liked anyone like this before." He smiled then quickly added, "Tell her I said any of that and I will kill you!" he threatened half-heartedly, but Nick did not think there was any intent and besides, after what he had just said, Nick was grinning ear to ear. Joe couldn't help but smile back. "Give her time, let her come to you, don't rush her. I didn't tell you that either!" At Freddy shouting across the yard, Joe slapped him on the arm and returned to Freddy, who was now grilling him about what had been said.

Leaving her alone would not be easy, not that he could find her even if he wanted to. Mel had the ability to just disappear, even in this tiny village. Every bone in his body ached to see her again; he couldn't think, his mind was a blur. Nick hadn't managed to get any writing done since he had arrived at Pine Tree Cottage, Melissa would have his guts for garters if he didn't get something done. He had promised her a sequel in exchange for time off but that had not happened yet, and since he couldn't see Mel for a few days he decided to try writing once more. Making a pot of tea, his new favourite thing to do, he sat at his computer, expecting his mind to be blank as it had been many times before. Changing tactics, he decided to try writing a new story rather than plump for the expected sequel. Far from the anticipated block, he found words flowing from him like a river, pouring out onto the screen. He wrote about delightful ladies in tea rooms, strong fathers guarding their children, and about a beautiful woman defending her life. He wrote long into the day and, without realising it, into the night.

A clanking noise abruptly woke him, his head marked from the keys that had imprinted into his forehead as he had slumped asleep on the keyboard. "I thought the country was supposed to be quiet," he complained out loud.

"Sorry, can't find anything," a voice replied. Nick shook his head, wondering if he was still asleep. Mel appeared from the kitchen carrying two plates of pasta. "Hope you don't mind, figured by the breakfast pots still in the sink that you hadn't eaten, and I am famished, I've been in the pub all day, they are doing out the cellar and needed help." Nick blinked heavily, trying to comprehend what was happening. "Your door was open," she explained, placing the pasta in front of him.

"I... must have fallen asleep," he said dopily. "I got carried away in my writing." His stomach let out a loud grumble, reminding him that he hadn't eaten since breakfast. Mel chuckled and handed him a fork. "Mmm this looks delicious." He hungrily scooped up the pasta, wondering where she had managed to find all the ingredients in his little kitchen.

"Joe taught me how to cook, not that you had much to work with, he is amazing, my dad. He said you had stopped by." She tilted her head, gauging his reaction. Nick swallowed hard.

"Oh yeah, what else did he say?" He felt panicked now, her eyes searching for answers.

"Just that you wanted to go out or something and that Freddy gave you a hard time." Nick let out a relieved sigh.

"I know he is your dad, well one of them, but I tell you, he scares the living daylights out of me."

Mel continued eating, obviously satisfied with his answer.

"Can I ask what you were writing?" She pointed to the screen filled with his work, he turned and suddenly had an awful thought that he had not saved it and did so quickly. It would not be the first time that he had lost entire stories, just because he was stupid enough to not click on the save button. Job done, he turned back to Mel, who sat expectantly.

"I guess I'm just writing about my experiences here," he began, "People I have met, the village, I

mean it's a writer's dream here, it's   so
beautiful and rich. I think I have fallen in love." Mel's
eyebrows shot up. "...Erm, with the village, I mean,
and the people," he corrected.

"So am I in there?" she asked him teasingly.

"In there? Mel, you are the whole story," he
replied, reaching for her hand and stroking it softly.
"Everything that happens from now on is all down
to you and your beautiful face, your loving nature,
everything that is you." He smiled as Mel sat
stunned by his words, the sincerity of them hanging
before her like a thick fog. "So you wanna go for a
drink or something?" he asked, "I can be ready in
two minutes." Mel burst into laughter; what was it
with this girl, always laughing at him?

"You might want to check the time, Nick," she
snorted.

"Oh my God, it's one in the morning!" he
exclaimed, looking at the clock on his computer
screen, how long had he been asleep? "You came
here at this time?" he asked her, puzzled.

"I said I was in the pub, I came here when it
closed, saw the light from your computer screen so
came in." He shook his head in amazement, so happy
to see her, just as Joe had advised him, she had come
back. "So are you still tired?" she asked suggestively,
he shook his head slowly. "Good," she smiled and,
taking his hand, led him up the stairs.

Nick's head whirled, was he rushing this? Was it too soon? Mel stopped at the top of the stairs then held her hand forward, suggesting he show her which room was his.

"Wow, you have a bath in your bedroom!" she shrieked excitedly. "That is so cool."

"That's how to kill the mood," he mocked her. Mel turned and looked from him to the bed. He strolled across the room, desperately trying to remain cool and casual. Not an easy feat when he could hardly breathe, his heart threatening to burst straight out of his chest, not to mention his trousers that were now cutting off his blood supply. Sitting down on the edge of the bed he patted the space next to him, Mel obliged, her eyes never leaving his. "You don't have to do this," he told her, he needed her to know there was no pressure.

"Now who's killing the mood?" she chastised, Mel stood up and moved to stand between Nick's legs, God, she was beautiful, so interesting, so unique. She made him feel like a different person, he was relaxed around her, comfortable with who he was. She did not want the author or the fame; she was just interested in him. He raised his hands and slid them up over her thighs to her waist, pulling her to him. She squealed, lost balance and fell onto him, both laughing as they tumbled onto the bed. "I'm trying to be sexy here, Nick," she pouted.

"You are, Mel, you don't need to try. You are sexy and beautiful and funny and smart and caring, all the time." If only he could tell her the whole truth, tell her that he had fallen head over heels in love with her, that he wanted to pack up and move to the village to spend every second with her. But that would scare her, push her away and he couldn't bear the thought of losing her.

"Nick, are you OK?" Mel asked, concerned at the sudden glumness in his eyes. He didn't answer, he turned and kissed her, if he couldn't tell her he would show her.

Mel sat up, raised her T-shirt up over her head, then reached around to undo her bra.

"Don't." Nick stopped her. "Let me, but not yet," his voice was low and sultry, he needed to savour this, take his time. He removed his own T-shirt and pulled her into his lap once more, his bare chest pressed against her warm flesh, the sensations rippling through him. His hand slid around her waist, up her back and held her firm, his mouth hungrily kissing hers.

Mel sat back, panting "Have I upset you? Is there any reason for you to be torturing me like this?" Her face was red, flushed, and Nick grinned smugly. Lowering his hands, he snapped her bra with one flick, Mel gasped, shocked at the sudden freedom. His cockiness vanished as he glided the straps down her arm. The delicate tattoo up her back carried on over her shoulder and down between her breasts, a fragile little buttercup nestled between them. Once again Nick froze, mesmerised by the little flower.

Mel took one of his hands and lifted it up, placing it directly over her left breast and holding it in place. God, he felt like a teenager again, his hand shaking like he had never touched a woman before. His mouth grew dry as Mel's own hand moved away from his and over to her right breast, showing him exactly what she needed him to do. He slowly, somehow, regained some sort of control and began to move, slowly circling her breasts leaning forward, needing to kiss that little buttercup. Mel moaned as his lips met her oversensitive skin. She had not been expecting him to kiss her there, it was gentle and chaste.

He wanted to touch her, touch her everywhere, trace the tattoos from start to end, every little detail of her. Never had it been like this with another woman, he had been involved with a few girls before but this, this was something else and it scared him to pieces.

Mel began to unbutton Nick's jeans, each pull as the button was released was blissful agony until finally she released him, he wore no shorts. Slowly Mel rolled his jeans down, standing to pull them off completely, followed by his socks. She stood before him, her voluptuous breasts free of their restraints were magnificent, her eyes glinting in acknowledgement as Nick's mouth watered for her. Sliding her hands into the side of her pants, she allowed them to fall to the floor, leaving her totally naked. Taking his time was no longer an option, he needed her, now! Catching her by surprise, he clambered up onto his knees and grabbed her, throwing her onto the bed.

"Nick!" she called out, but Nick silenced her with a kiss.

"Mel, I'm sorry, I will apologise for this in the morning but right now I need you," and with that he shrugged and kissed her, forcing his tongue into her mouth, tasting her, drawing her in more and more. With minimal effort he reached to the side to grab his wallet, never relinquishing his kiss and grabbed a condom, one that had been in there for over a year, but never mind. Once protected, he gazed into her eyes, struggling to restrain this carnal desire that was invading him. "Are you OK?" he asked feebly, Mel took his hand and placed it between her legs.

"Shit," he growled, if he wasn't ready to go before, he was now. He could feel how excited she was, how turned on. In one stroke he pushed himself inside, at once feeling like he had entered heaven, Mel gasped her approval and Nick lost himself, lost himself in the moment, lost himself in Mel.

He should be taking his time, he should be pleasing her, but he couldn't, he couldn't think, he just needed to take, to have this first time. His brain dissolved and nothing else mattered, nothing in the world existed but this moment, this feeling. All his good intentions vanished, his desire to take things slowly disappeared, he knew what he should do, but Mel had set a firework off inside him and now he couldn't stop.

Mel cried out as Nick continued his relentless pace, his need and desire exposed and raw in his eyes. He grabbed her by the waist and flipped them both so that he was lying on his back.

"You need to do it, I can't stop, Mel," he panted, still pushing into her, but she had no desire to slow things down, and gripping him firmly continued the assault. Nick began calling her name over and over, sending her into spasms of delight, gripping his shoulders to try and anchor herself to reality. She fell against his chest as he panted, unable to find a voice, and still connected they fell asleep in each other's arms.

Chapter 10

"I'M SO SORRY, Mel."

"Yes, you've already said that, Nick!"

"I know, but I am really, really sorry I don't know what got into me."

"Yes, you've already said that as well." Mel was now becoming annoyed with his apologising.

"I just…"

"Nick!" Mel interrupted. "For God sake, do you know what? Sometimes, just sometimes, women like fast and furious. Sometimes they quite enjoy it! Not all women want to 'make love' all the time." Nick hung his head in shame, he was so embarrassed about the night before. He had taken and not given a second thought to Mel's needs, he was so ashamed of himself.

"I promise it will be better next time," he assured her. Mel raised an eyebrow over her morning cup of tea.

"So you think there will be 'a next time' do you?" Then, seeing the look of horror on his face, realised he was in no joking mood. She put her cup down and walked over to him, cradling his head to her chest. "Nick, I will let you in on a little secret, what happened last night was not you being selfish or greedy. What happened was two people having a great time. Do you realise how sexy it was that you lost control? Nick, your face turned wild and your eyes...wow, your eyes." She leaned down and kissed his eyelids gently. Nick slowly began to relax, it had been a wild night, he had needed her so desperately, it had completely taken him by surprise. Now they were sitting here together having breakfast, and she wasn't running, in fact she seemed quite content to stay.

"I needed you so badly," he confessed quietly, Mel just grinned.

"I kind of got that."

"Erm," Nick began awkwardly "Did you...?"

"Jesus, Nick, do you always do this? Analyse everything, bloody hell. Am I the only one who thought last night was unbelievably amazing?" She was losing her temper with him now. Nick grabbed her before she could walk away and pulled her down into his lap.

"I wanted our first time to be special, that's all." Mel ran her finger across his face and kissed him.

"It was special, Nick; it was amazing and then some!" Immediately Nick felt the effects of her kissing him, of where she was sitting, and shuffled her back to sit on his legs instead. What was happening to him? Every time she was near he

turned into a bumbling wreck, and
every time she so much as touched him, well ... it had
consequences.

"So, you kind of like me then?" Mel teased him, he
looked down at the growing bulge that was now
threatening to peek out through his robe.

"What do you think?" he asked, tilting his head in
amusement.

"I think you should take me back to bed," she
announced standing up.

"No work today?" he asked gleefully, almost
tripping up over his own feet to follow her up the
stairs.

"Nope, Mondays are always quiet, have to go to
the café later but this morning...erm?" She glanced
up to the ceiling, as if checking her schedule. "Nope,
nothing, I guess I can squeeze you in." She
suggestively licked her lips. 'Right,' Nick thought,
'This time I do it properly! '

Mel stretched out lazily in the bath whilst Nick
lay on the bed reading his newspapers, but every
now and then he glanced over to watch this most
beautiful creature soaking in his bath. How had this
happened? He wasn't looking for love, and yet here
she was right next to him.

"This may be the best idea anyone has ever had,"
Mel mused, the bubbles covering her like a fluffy

blanket. "Do you think I could fit a bath in my place?" Nick snorted.

"I don't think you could fit a TV in your place," he mocked. Mel shot him a disgusted look.

"My dad did that for me, I love it," she snapped, Nick had crossed a line and he knew it. Mel was furiously protective of her fathers.

"I'm sorry, it's a lovely place, I just meant it is small that's all." Her face calmed a little "And that's good for me because it means anytime you want a long, hot bath you will want to come here." He folded his paper and moved to the side of the bath. Picking up the wash cloth he slowly began bathing her shoulders in the wonderfully warm water. She groaned at his touch.

"Anytime I want?" she murmured. Nick smiled, visions of living here with Mel flashed through his mind, making a home together, always having her with him, forever. He didn't reply, just continued to allow the water to flow in small steady streams over her shoulders as he daydreamed about the life he wanted to have with her. He had shown her just how much he loved her this morning, taken his time, worshipped her body the way she deserved. When she finally cried out his name over and over and her body had shaken with the powerful climax, Nick had told her he loved her, very quietly and softly into her neck. She didn't hear him, her panting so loud he didn't hear himself, but he told her and he meant it,

he loved her with all his heart and
soul. The question now was, what to do about it?

The sun shone brightly as the day moved on, Nick and Mel still lay in bed and there was nowhere else in the world he wanted to be. His whole body felt alive, tingling, every hair standing on end like his senses were on red alert. Sighing loudly, he relaxed and stretched out, elongating every muscle, offering the release they all craved, he couldn't remember feeling this good, even when he had had a full body massage. Mel was amazing; she seemed to anticipate his every need, every desire. Making love to Mel had been a first time experience for him, he had never made love before because that is what they had done, not just had sex, they had loved each other. There had been no rush, they had all day to just be with each other, explore each other's bodies.

"Really?" Mel murmured as she felt Nick's excitement pressing up to the small of her back where he had scooted up to. Even the memories excited him, he was insatiable.

"Well, if you're awake?" He kissed her shoulder and gradually made his way up her neck, nuzzling into her hairline, she groaned softly and the sound was enough to push him over the edge. "You are so beautiful, Mel," Nick professed as he traced his way down the delicate trail of buttercups that twisted their way down her spine to her delectable round backside. She shivered a little as he tickled her.

"Nick, knock it off for goodness sake! We have been in bed all day!" she chuckled, pulling the blankets back ready to stand up, but Nick was having none of it and held her tightly.

"So?"

"So! It's not normal and I am hungry." Nick groaned and pouted like a child, Mel shook her head and threw her pillow at him, then kissed him. The gentle kiss she had intended to give him very quickly progressed, and Nick's hands were on her again, twisting in her hair, the silk strands weaving around each finger. Mel's hands stroked his cheek then smoothly moved down to rest on his chest, his pecs firm and solid. Her stomach growled loudly and Nick smiled against her lips, and just like that his excitement faded as his need to care for her took over.

"Scrambled eggs and a ham toastie for the lady?" Nick proudly placed the plate in front of Mel as she descended the staircase, her makeup and hair firmly in place.

"Wow, you sure know how to treat a girl!" she mocked, he smacked her hand with the spatula that was in his hand.

"Don't be sarcastic, missus, there is not a lot in the cupboards as you seem to frequently point out!"

The two sat at the kitchen table and ate their meal in silence, neither one feeling the need to speak, just giving the occasional grin as they looked up from their plate and saw the other one looking as well. Nick felt so happy, never before had he felt so relaxed and comfortable, his worries of the last few months seemed miles away and a life time ago. With Mel the world seemed a better place, he just didn't care about the little things that used to niggle him, they seemed insignificant now. He was in love and falling deeper and deeper every second he was with her.

"Has anyone ever told you, you are so slow at getting ready?" Mel tapped her nails impatiently on the table as she waited for Nick.

"What's the rush? It's not like you are working for Alice and Rose today and it is practically night now anyway!" Mel just huffed; annoyed with the time it was taking to get his pert backside out of the door.

"Maybe I should just go on my own," she teased as she stood to leave.

"No! no I'm here look, all ready," he panicked as he rushed down the stairs nearly tripping over, there was no way he wanted her to leave, he had just decided that he loved her without a doubt and there was no way he wanted to leave her side for more than a second.

Though it was late in the afternoon the sun pounded down ferociously as they strolled hand in hand up the nightmare of a hill to the café. Mel watched him, concerned, as he paused once to take a breath of his inhaler.

"Please don't watch me do this" he uttered, embarrassed by her expression. Mel took the inhaler from his hand and kissed his lips, then moved down to kiss his throat.

"Don't ever, ever, be embarrassed about this, Nick." She held up his inhaler. "This is a symbol, it shows that you battle every day and that you win, it is not a sign of weakness, it is a sign of strength." Nick stared at the small blue inhaler that had caused him so much humiliation as a child, that he had always tried to hide from people. Mel didn't see it like that, she saw the world in a different way to everyone else, if it was at all possible he fell in love with her all over again. He smiled, putting the inhaler back into his pocket, and took her hand once more.

"So..." Mel began as they resumed walking "...how come you don't need that in the bedroom?" Nick snorted.

"What?"

"Well, I mean, you do far more aerobic stuff in the bedroom than a gentle stroll uphill but you don't use it then!" Mel giggled

"I don't believe you sometimes! I really don't."

"I'm just curious," she looked up into his eyes again. "Do you need it, but don't do it?" Nick suddenly realised the worry behind the joking.

"Baby, yes, you take my breath away every time I see you, let alone touch you but I don't know, it's a different kind of breathing. I can't explain it, but I promise you, if I ever need it I will take it. Please don't worry." Mel smiled, satisfied, and Nick got a warm feeling as he saw this beautiful creature whom he had known a few short days care so much for him.

Chapter 11

"ABOUT TIME!" ROSE scolded as Nick and Mel finally fell through the café door. Rose could not hide her joy at seeing the two of them together. "Here, you carry this!" She shoved a basket into Nick's hand and began locking up the café.

"A picnic at this time?" Nick asked curiously. Rose just continued to lock the door and gave him a dirty look; Mel sniggered at his hurt expression and squeezed his hand tightly. Rose set the pace as they headed over the other side of the hill away from the village, away from the sparse houses and into the endless hills and fields that lay in front of them.

"It so beautiful here," Nick announced as he gazed at the beautiful countryside around him. "We just don't have anything like this, I mean I went to parks and stuff when I was little but nothing like this." Rose smiled and told him that it had not changed since she was a little girl; yes, there were a few more houses built and larger shops on the outskirts but inside the village, time had stood still.

"What's going on over there? Nick asked as he saw movement over in the far lane.

"It's the army, they do a lot of training here, you get used to it," Mel explained. There was a base not too far away and so tanks, soldiers and gunfire had become a part of their life now. Every so often flares could be seen as they completed overnight missions, or tanks would come hurling down the side roads, but no one ever gave it a second thought anymore. That was the strange thing about country life, no matter how strange or bizarre life was, if it was around long enough, it just became accepted.

Rose suddenly stopped talking and turned to Nick; she grabbed the basket from his hands and gave it to Mel, who immediately fell a few steps behind. At Nick's bemused face, Mel just smiled and nodded to him, indicating that he should go on with Rose who was now taking his arm and walking a little bent.

"Are you OK, Rose?" Nick asked, now getting worried at the old lady's change in stance.

"Yes, yes, come on come on," she chanted out almost gleefully. As they rounded the corner of the winding road Nick came face to face with a soldier in full army gear, the shock made him stop in his tracks. Rose nodded to the sergeant, who nodded back silently then, grabbing Nick's arm tighter, pulled him on. Along the side of the road were more soldiers, trainees, Nick presumed, all on their knees, all facing the stone wall that lined the road. "They're training," Rose explained "gets really annoying when you are having a lovely walk and a bloody great big tank comes hurtling along the road!" she muttered under her breath. "Still, they pay for the roads and stuff so I suppose there are advantages, they have to reinforce them you see, to take the weight." Nick tried hard to listen but all he saw was

the endless line of men, some his
age and some not much older than boys, all facing
towards the wall away from them. "Was this a
punishment?" he wondered.

"At least it's nice weather, eh!" Nick called out,
hoping to make the poor sad faces on the boys lift a
little.

"Nice weather?" the sergeant shouted out, "What
do you think to that, lads?"

All the boys then shouted out in unison, "If it ain't
raining, it ain't training!" and immediately returned
to their silent pose.

"Rose!" Mel called out as Rose suddenly began to
waver on her feet, Nick grasped the arm that was
linked in his and tried to help her remain standing.
The sergeant was at his side in an instant.

"Has she eaten or drank?" he began

"I'm fine, fine, I just went a little dizzy, that's all
really." She tried to stand again but wobbled, and
the two men held her again. Nick turned to ask Mel
if she had a drink in the basket but he held his
tongue fast. Mel had opened the basket and quick as
a flash was handing things out to the boys, who
were rapidly stuffing things into their pockets! Rose
dug her elbow into his side, forcing him to return his
attention to her as she gave him a stern look and
began to speak like a frail old lady.

"Maybe I should call for support," the sergeant offered, but before he could turn to issue the instruction, Rose miraculously gained some strength in her legs and began to stand.

"Oh thank you, young man. I don't know what came over me, really I don't."

"Mmm, I can't think!" Nick mumbled sarcastically. Rose just smiled sweetly as Mel came up behind her.

"Come on, Rose, maybe we should abandon our walk and head home." Mel repeated her obviously rehearsed lines.

"I think that would be best, ma'am," the sergeant agreed.

As soon as they were out of earshot, Nick let rip. "What the hell was that all about?" he roared but Rose and Mel went into a fit of hysterics. "I was worried, Rose," he added, wanting to make them both feel bad.

"I am sorry, Nick," Rose offered. "Really I am."

"Rose and I have been doing this for years; I mean it's just heartbreaking to watch them all. You saw how young they were, some of these boys have never even been away from home before." Mel hated seeing the boys like this, she understood that they had to be trained, but when the army came to the village it was with new recruits, "Hell week they call it," she told him.

"It's not like we are interfering with their training, just offering a little morale boost," Rose justified, and opening the basket gave Nick one of the packets Mel had been handing out to the boys behind their sergeant's back. "Just a flapjack, full of sugar, nuts, fruit, a little energy boost."

Nick had to agree; they tasted good and did give him that little energy boost to get back up the hill to the café.

Reaching the café they said their goodbyes, and Rose disappeared off into the little cottage located behind the café.

"Now what?" Nick asked Mel. "Go free some animals from a laboratory?"

"Ha ha, the man suddenly finds a sense of humour!" Mel retorted.

"You have a big heart, Mel." Nick curled Mel's stray hair around her ear, she amazed him at every turn. Every time he thought he had begun to scratch the surface with her, she just shocked him with something else.

"Come on then, out with it!" she demanded, examining his expression. He smiled affectionately. "Look, Rose and I have done that forever, I just thought you would like to see part of our life and they are part of our life. They come and they go, they train and they leave, it's sad to see all the boys struggling, but it also gives me such a sense of pride to think that we are, in some small way, helping," she stuttered "I don't know...it's just...I don't know. It's silly, I guess".

Nick silenced her with a kiss, he loved her so deeply, she saw the world in a unique way, a way he simply hadn't seen it before and he wanted to be in every single part of it. Mel had again shared a moment with him, an experience that he guessed no one had shared with her before. Every time she shared these things she was showing him a trust, a belief that he would not run away from her, but also that she had no desire to run from him. These little gestures were Mel's way of telling him she loved him. Nick smiled and squeezed her hand tightly, losing himself in her beautiful eyes for just a moment before they went on their way. She was sharing her life with him.

"Come on, as you have no food I guess we will have to eat at the pub tonight" Nick grinned, having spent the day in bed with Mel and then handing out treats to the young soldiers, the evening had crept up on him.

"And then?" he asked hopefully but didn't dare to presume.

"And then, what?" Mel asked, faking innocence.

"And then?" he asked more sternly, pulling her body against him, his hunger for food suddenly turning into hunger for something entirely different.

"And then we go home," she smiled sweetly, and Nick's heart exploded into a million happy little pieces.

"Shall I walk you to the pub?" Nick asked as Mel got dressed the next day, ready to go to work at the pub. She had clothes and make up all stashed in the little rucksack she always carried.

"You don't have to," she called out from the bathroom. No he didn't have to, but he wanted to. He wanted to find out every little detail about Mel, everything that made her who she was, her likes and dislikes, he couldn't find out enough. By the time they had managed to get out of bed, the morning had long gone and it was now lunchtime, and Mel had to be at the pub for the afternoon and evening shift whilst their usual bar staff were on holiday. They sat in the lounge eating lunch as Nick couldn't face sitting out in the garden any more, it had lost its glory for him since the day he came home to the chicken bloodbath. He talked about his family and Uncle George in particular. Mel talked about her fathers and how wonderful they were, her different jobs and how she loved her freedom. It started Nick thinking, and he worried that she might not want a relationship or the commitment of being tied to one man.

"Come on, then." Mel nipped his arm waking him up from his daydream "Are you walking me there then or what?" Nick grinned and grabbed his keys. Leaving the car, they walked hand in hand up and over the ridge towards the pub. "Oh great!" Mel sighed, "the hikers are all in." Nick understood exactly what she meant; they were lovely people, just a bit full on, so to speak.

As they opened the doors to the pub he immediately stopped. Mel squeezed his hand so tightly he thought she would stop the blood. Two men stood over at the bar talking to Julian, who looked very nervous, Mel refused to move; instead she was rooted to the spot.

"Who are you?" one of the men asked gruffly. "You locals?" His intense stare turned to Mel, who backed away slightly, Nick grabbed her hand to pull her protectively next to him.

"I could ask the same of you," Nick retaliated, Julian silently and subtly shook his head, all the locals looked petrified and many of them were staring at Mel nervously. The two men looked at each other.

"I guess she would be about the right age?" one of them said to the other.

"Surely not, not a very good disguise is it, she don't exactly fit him." The man snorted at his own humour and Nick felt Mel's hand tighten once more. Nick looked around and saw all the hikers, completely oblivious as to the drama unfolding around them.

"Morning," Nick called out brightly. "Heading up to Heavens Point today?" Heavens Point was a spot right at the top of one of the peaks, it was a really hard trek to get there but Mel had said that the views were spectacular. The hikers all turned to him.

"Afternoon, I think you will find," a jolly man replied. "Didn't see you this morning?"

"No but we heard you!" the other man chortled and all the others laughed. The hikers were staying in various cottages around Nick, he blushed in embarrassment. "So what are you, newlyweds or something?" the man asked.

"Engaged," Nick lied, Mel nodded behind him, trying to play along.

"Thought as much, you should join us this afternoon, it's gonna be a good one." He returned to his drink, chatting with all the other hikers about weather etc, oblivious to what was happening around him. Nick returned his attention to the two men.

"So, you tourists?" the larger man confirmed. Nick just nodded.

"What is all this about?" he asked, the two men stood and walked over to the door, obviously satisfied with the answer they had given.

"Best if you just keep your nose out and move on, pal!" the man whispered into Nick's ear, he cringed and every hair on his arm stood to attention.

When Nick was sure they had completely gone, he opened the pub front door to see a car driving away.

"What the hell was that all about?" he asked the entire pub. "Mel, are you OK?" Mel was still frozen to the spot; the colour had drained from her already pale face. One of the locals spoke out.

"I've called Joe and Fred, they're on their way, girl, you'd best run," and it was like a light had been switched on in Mel's head, she looked at Nick and then ran out of the door.

"Wait, Mel!" Nick called out, running after her. She was quick, she was already down the road and Nick struggled to keep up. A large truck screeched to a halt inches away from her, and dust and gravel flew up obscuring Nick's view. As she climbed in and slammed the door he saw it was Joe and Freddy, he called out to her but she didn't reply. Reaching the truck before it left, he banged on the window. "What the hell? Who were those men, Mel?" Freddy rolled down the window.

"Stay out of this boy, it's no concern of yours." Nick turned to Joe in the hope of a little support but Joe just nodded his head in agreement. Nick stood aghast as the truck sped off at top speed. Nick didn't delay, he turned heels and ran straight back to the pub.

Nell put a drink in front of him but he couldn't face it. "I need to know what's going on!" he demanded. The locals wouldn't talk to him, most of them had already left by the time he returned.

"I really don't know," Nell replied honestly. "They still don't accept us in the village and we have lived here for years." She reached out and rubbed his hand caringly. "All I know is that every couple of years these blokes come in looking for a local girl, we were told to say nothing when they come, so that's what we do."

"I had no idea it was Mel they were looking for," Julian joined in.

"No, me neither," Nell answered her husband. Nick's heart broke, he didn't like unanswered questions, and this was about Mel. She was in danger, he could feel it. Something was very, very wrong and someone must know what was going on. Julian took pity on him.

"Come on, I will give you a lift," he offered. Nell looked at her husband in shock.

"What are you doing?" she asked.

"Look at him, he's a mess, he has the right to know and I don't care how big those men are, they are going to tell him." Julian puffed his chest out and Nick shot out of his seat.

As they pulled into the farmyard Nick could already see it was deserted, the truck and car had gone, the animals were all locked up in the barns and the Jack Russell pups were nowhere to be seen.

"She's gone!" Nick cried out, his heart shattered, the desperation and despair drowning him, he might never see her again. Why was he feeling so strong about her? He had only just met her, why did he care so much? Mel was obviously trouble with a capital T and he really did not need to get mixed up in anything, but he couldn't just stand back. Something had happened, he had fallen in love with her and he needed her safe and with him. It was his job now, he felt it, he needed to keep her safe and from harm, however she felt about him was irrelevant, he was lost to her.

"Look, they may have just gone off for a few days, they wouldn't leave the farm, Nick," Julian tried to assure him. "Come on, let's go back to the pub, have a few drinks."

"Thanks," Nick replied despondently, "but I just want to go home."

Chapter 12

NICK DIDN'T GO to bed that night, he stayed on the sofa listening to every bump or creak thinking, hoping, that Mel would come back to him. His mind raced, he really didn't understand what had happened. He had had the most amazing morning with Mel, it had been incredible and she had stayed with him, talked to him, loved him. But then those two men had turned up. Nick knew the look, they were not good men. The scars on their faces and the way the smaller man kept reaching into his jacket told Nick they were not looking for her to wish her well; they were going to hurt her. But why? Mel had lived in the village all her life, what could she have possibly done to cause these nasty thugs to be looking for her?

He had slept on and off all night, every little noise rousing him, his heart lurching, hoping it was her, but it was now light and he was still alone. His phone rang, causing him to jump.

"Hello?"

"Nick, it's Nell, I just wanted to check you were OK," Nell asked in a concerned tone.

"Any news?" Nick asked hopefully but no, no news. He convinced her that he was OK and told her he would call her again this afternoon, not forgetting to remind her to call him if there was any news at all.

"Nick, I have been trying to talk to the locals with no luck, but Alice was really off with me when I asked her about it. I don't know, it may be nothing but I just got the impression she knew more than she was letting on." Nick jumped up excitedly, it may be nothing but it may be something, and he rushed upstairs to get dressed. At least he would be doing something rather than just sitting in the cottage, waiting, imagining all sorts of awful possibilities.

As he reached the café Nick's head spun and he began to feel dizzy, he had taken the hill at a run and now his breathing was short and he just couldn't pull enough oxygen into his lungs. He had left his inhaler behind in his excitement at finally being proactive, not to mention the car that sat unused outside the cottage, but now he fought to take in any air around him. He tried in vain to slow his breathing, forcing himself to hold his breath then slowly release it. "Calm down, don't panic," he told himself over and over again, but he was losing the battle. His legs buckled beneath him and he blacked out, the sight of Rose running towards him going fuzzy and out of focus.

"Don't be ridiculous, Rose, Jesus, you have this romantic view of the world, WAKE UP!"

"Alice, he needs to know," Rose was shouting.

"We took an oath," Alice was reminding her.

"LOOK AT HIM!" Rose blurted out.

Nick's eyes fluttered open as he listened to the two old ladies, his breath was slowly returning to normal. "Maybe his mum was right after all, maybe it was just panic attacks that he suffered from now and the asthma he suffered from as a child was decreasing. He forced his breath in and out, regulating it, and tried to swallow but his mouth was so dry. He felt a glass pushed to his lips and the cold feeling of water filled his mouth, Nick drank it down greedily, black spots darting around in front of his eyes.

"When was the last time you ate, lad?" Rose asked kindly. Nick shook his head, he really couldn't remember. Rose and Alice helped him to his feet and walked him into the café; Alice disappeared into the kitchen and returned with a plateful of ham and eggs. He knew he had to eat but his stomach was refusing. Rose took his knife and fork and began cutting up his food.

"Please don't make me do the choo choo train," she chuckled. Nick smiled weakly and took the fork from her hand.

"Thank you," he muttered. "This is lovely and very kind of you," he added to Alice, who was standing in the doorway with her arms folded across her chest, her severe expression pasted on her face.

"My own hen's eggs," she uttered eventually, "Old Ben's pig an' all, all fresh from round here, no artificial nonsense," she lifted her chin proudly.

"You can tell, it's great." Nick attempted to be polite but returned to look at Rose, desperately begging her to tell him something, anything. However, it was Alice who spoke up.

"It ain't right you doing this, Rose, I will play no part," and she strutted off into the kitchen.

"Please," Nick began.

"You eat first, then I will talk," Rose insisted. Nick gobbled the food down in record time, his stomach turning it over and over until he felt sick. He sipped water and tried to keep the food from returning all over the table.

When Rose was satisfied that he was OK and no longer dizzy, she suggested that they sit outside, not forgetting to bring his water with them.

"We were all in the town hall that night, well the older village members, having a town meeting you see," she twisted her hands together nervously, Nick reached over.

"I promise, I will never pass on what you tell me today." He tried to show her that he meant it, that he was honest and trustworthy.

"I know, dear, I know, I wouldn't be telling you any of this if I thought anything else of you," she smiled.

Joe and Freddy had burst into the town hall that night; Joe had a baby cradled in his arms. They explained that they had found a car in a ditch crashed into the side of one of their fields, there was a woman in the car about to give birth. They had helped as best as they could but the mother had died within minutes of the baby being born. As the woman was dying she had asked the men to take care of her baby, had told them that people were looking for her and they were to keep her safe.

"I tell you, it was a shock," Rose recalled. "Some wanted to call the police, some said we shouldn't get involved."

"And what did you think?" Nick asked, Rose sighed

"It wasn't hard, I took one look at Joe holding that tiny, little girl in his arms, his eyes were all lit up like a Christmas tree, I knew exactly where that little girl needed to be." She smiled fondly. "He fell in love with her the minute he saw her; Freddy, however, took a bit of convincing but he was always protective of Joe. He was worried about them getting into trouble but he always gave into Joe, did whatever made Joe happy."

"Did the police ever find out?" Nick asked, Rose shook her head, the nearest police station was in the next town and unless something big happened they never ventured this far into the Dales.

"To be honest, the man in charge at the time was not the sharpest tool in the shed anyway," Rose admitted. They had spun a story about Freddy having a one night stand with a woman - resulting in Mel, and that the mother had just turned up on the doorstep, leaving Mel with him. It had given them an excuse as to why they had no paperwork for Mel, and to everyone other than the people who were in the village hall that night, it seemed plausible.

Nick still did not understand why these men were looking for Mel's mother. Why were they still looking for Mel? But that was all that Rose knew, the villagers had kept Mel hidden but men came every few years looking for her, she didn't know why, she had just kept the promise that she had made years ago.

"I'm sorry I can't tell you more, dear," Rose apologised, "If I hear anything I will tell you though, I promise." Nick nodded.

"Thanks, and thanks for the food, my wallet and money is at home, can I pay you later?" Rose waved her hand dismissively.

"Nonsense, it's on the house, boy. Now you make sure you eat properly, you won't be any good if you get ill, will you?" She hugged Nick and told him not to worry, that she was sure Mel would be back in a day or two.

Nick took the walk back slowly, he missed Mel, wanted her safe with him; he knew Freddy and Joe would never let anything happen to Mel but he wanted her with him. Not knowing where she was, was killing him. Taking Rose's advice he stopped by the local store to collect some snacks. Mr Michaels ran the shop, and was furiously piling things up onto the counter.

"Hi." Nick mustered up all the energy he had to try and sound cheerful, Mr Michaels nodded in return. Nothing grabbed his fancy, he had no appetite, but Rose was right, he needed his strength, he grabbed a few bread rolls and some ham. Mr Michaels' gaze followed him round as he looked at the stock. Nick couldn't get to anything else as it was all behind the counter, he suspected this was so that no one would mess up Mr Michaels' meticulous displays. He asked for some crisps and cereal bars, then suddenly remembered that he had no cash on him. Scratching his forehead, exhausted and fed up, he confessed his error. Mr Michaels frowned before allowing Nick to set up an account, but exaggerated the fact that each account needed to be paid in full at the end of the week. Nick thanked him and left.

The day just got better and better, Nick thought, as he put his shopping away in the cupboards. Now what was he supposed to do, just sit around and wait? He turned on his laptop and re-read the writing he had done before Mel had come to visit. It was good, he couldn't be modest, the story and the characters were gripping and interesting, but they were fiction and he needed the real thing. Tears began to fall as he sat staring at the screen, not able to read anything through the blurred vision.

"Damn it, I can't do it!" he raged, leaping to his feet. "I can't just sit here." There was only place he could go, maybe she wasn't there but it was the only place he could think of going. The farm wasn't far, only ten minutes' walk, in the car he could be there in no time at all. At least he would be doing something.

"Joining us after all then?" the hikers called out as they saw Nick leaving.

"Oh erm not today, sorry."

"Where is that lovely fiancée of yours today?" they called out cheerily. But Nick could not answer, his tears had begun to fall again and he had to get out of there before he had a full breakdown. Each step he took towards his car made him feel sick, was she there? Was she OK? What if she wasn't there?

The yard still looked empty, no truck or car was parked in front of the barns, and Nick felt hopeless, darkness filling his every thought. Not knowing what to do next, he began to stroll around the yard, kicking rocks out of his way in frustration. As his rock hit the barn door he heard whimpering; frowning, he moved closer to the door. Frantic barking then greeted him, this must be where the

Jack Russell pups were locked up
but there was another noise, a whining noise.

"Sshh now, sshh, dogs," he called out through the door, and pressed his ear straining to hear the noise again. Yes, there it was, it was definitely a whimper, something was hurt. "Shit," Nick cursed out loud. The barn was locked with a padlock; he walked around looking for loose boards, anything to help him get in. The whining increased, and the pups began the stressful barking again, Nick couldn't stand it anymore. Choosing a loose panel he kicked with all his might, putting his foot straight through the wood. A few more kicks saw a hole large enough for Nick to put his head in to see inside. The three pups barked loudly but would not move, a few more kicks and Nick managed to squeeze himself through.

"Shit!" he called out as he felt pain in his shoulder, a sharp piece of wood now jutted out of it. "Sshh now, come on let me see." He shooed the dogs to one side. Another dog lay on the floor, he presumed it was the pups' mother, the way they had circled her. "Come on now, shift." He gently placed his foot under Fatso's belly, not wanting to risk his fingers by putting them anywhere near the yapping, distressed dog, and slowly edged him away. "Oh, God," Nick exclaimed, as a very pregnant dog lay panting. His heart raced, he knew nothing about dogs, let alone dogs giving birth. He took off his shirt and laid it over the dog, she turned her head as though begging him to help her, then let out another long whine, her pain obvious to him. He tried to get the little dogs out of the way and one by one pushed them through the gap he had created, eventually they scampered off. Nick returned to the mother, who was shaking, he looked around the barn for something to help, anything. As he stroked the dog's head gently, talking to her in hushed tones, the barn door flew open, on the other side stood Mel.

Chapter 13

Nick was torn in two, he wanted to run to Mel, hold her in his arms but this dog needed him, she was in excruciating pain and whimpering in his arms. Mel's eyes darted first to Nick and then to the dog, the panic showing in her eyes.

"What happened?" she cried out, rushing to the dog's side. "Oh my God!"

Nick reached out to comfort her. "Thank God you're alright, Mel, please don't ever run out on me again," he pleaded.

"Nick I..." she began, but the dog's cry silenced her, horrified, she looked to Nick.

"Where's Freddy or Joe?" Nick asked, hoping they weren't far away.

"They went to town," Mel sobbed.

"There must be a phone, some way of contacting them?" but Mel just shook her head, Nick needed to think.

"The pub! Ring Julian and Nell, then call Mr Michaels, then Rose and Alice. One of them will find them. Mel...MEL!" he called out but Mel was in shock. She had raised this dog, watched her give birth to the three Jack Russell's barking outside not two years ago. There had been no problems then but she was older now. Mel sobbed hysterically. "Mel, the dog needs you, I need you, I can't do this on my own, you have to get help!" Mel came to her senses and set off to the house at a pace.

"OK, girl, it's OK, we are gonna do this," he soothed; suddenly the dog's stomach contracted and heaved. Nick reached around to see a small pink blob plop out onto the floor, he grabbed it and began clearing away all the mucus and afterbirth.

"Jeez, I've seen this on the TV, what did they do?" He wracked his brains "Rub!" That was it; they rub them upside down to get the lungs clear. Nick swung the puppy head down and began rubbing the back, to his delight the pup gave a sort of hiccup and squeaked loudly.

"Look, look we did it!" he cried joyfully, showing the dog her little pup; she gave it a little lick and began again. Nick put the pup onto her teats and looked for another. Again the little bundle came out and Nick repeated the process until the little pink pup squeaked. He waited to see if there were any more; the dog lying on the floor was still panting and crying. Taking a closer look he saw that there was one more, but for whatever reason it wasn't fully out. The mother just laid her head on the barn floor, panting slowly. She had given up, and Nick had no idea what to do about it. Nick sucked in his breath, trying not to lose his breakfast, and grabbed the pup, pulling slightly. The dog let out a howl and Nick immediately dropped it.

"Shoot," he panicked, he knew enough to know the pup had to come out, summoning all his courage he attempted again, the mother lifted her head and started to lick herself, slowly Nick felt the contractions around the pup start again. "Come on, girl, we can do this," he almost pleaded to her. The black puppy came out in one and Nick began rubbing just as Mel came skidding around the corner.

"Joe was at the shop, he's coming now, Freddy's gone for the vet!" she shouted "How is she?" She didn't see the two pups now suckling like pros, she only saw her dog panting slowly, not moving. She stroked the dog's head, tears pouring down her face. "Please, Millie, please be OK." But Nick was preoccupied, the little black pup was not hiccupping or coughing, it simply swung lifeless as he desperately rubbed its back. "Is it not breathing?" Mel asked, finally noticing Nick's attempts. Nick shook his head, his own tears now flowing in streams splashing onto the floor. "Oh God no, please, Nick, don't let it die, please." His heart broke as Mel wept. This had been her pet, her companion and now it was very possible she may lose her and the pup. A ghastly thought ran through Nick's mind, did Mel see her mother in this same scenario? Did she see her mother dying as she gave birth to her, just as this little dog was dying whilst giving birth to her pup? Mel cried, "Please don't let her die, Nick, Please. She can't die!" she begged, distraught.

"Mel!" a voice called out, running into the barn, Mel ran into Joe's arms. Joe very quickly assessed the situation.

"Mel, it happens, you know this. It's a runt, they often don't make it, we have to concentrate on Millie now. Go get some warm water and towels from the cupboard." Mel ran off obediently. "You OK?" he asked Nick, whose tear-stained face betrayed how he was feeling. "It's OK, Nick, you did your best. Sometimes there is just nothing you can do, but I have to concentrate on Millie. If this dog dies, it will break Mel's heart." Nick nodded, not giving up on the tiny pup in his hands. Just as Mel came running back in, Freddy ran in with the vet.

With one quick look at Joe, Freddy sent the vet straight over to Millie. Mel still sobbed hysterically, her tears falling over the dog's muzzle. Freddy strode over to Nick, took the pup from him and gave it one forceful swing downwards, then raised it to his face to listen to its tiny chest. Again he swung the pup down roughly by the legs, then delicately blew a tiny breath into the dog's face. Nick stood motionless, watching this big bear of a man work on the pup that in his hands looked more like a tiny mouse. Freddy opened the pup's mouth and cleared out the mucus, then made one final swing. He then threw the pup back into Nick's arms and ordered him to keep rubbing. Nick obeyed without question, finally releasing his held breath when he heard a tiny little cough from the pup, his heart leaping with joy. Freddy, expressionless, then turned his attentions to the vet.

"Get the oxygen from my car," the vet ordered Freddy, who didn't hesitate. The vet still monitored Millie, listening to her heart. Mel had her hands clamped firmly over her mouth, unable to control her sobbing, she had tried to quieten herself so that the vet could hear.

"Talk," he snarled out to Nick, who immediately explained quickly about hearing the crying, about the two pups coming easily and then about the runt getting stuck and Millie just giving up. The vet nodded and hummed with understanding.

"Change of plan, Fred!" the vet shouted, "Pack them all up and I will take them away with me."

Mel looked at him, horrified. "It's OK, just precautions. Millie will be fine, I promise, Mel," he comforted. "She needs rest and I need to get a drip into her to get her strength back." Freddy lifted Millie out to the car whilst Joe brought the pups who were now wriggling and grunting, wanting to get back to their mother.

Freddy put his arm around Mel as the vet drove off. "Come on, girl, you heard him, they will all be fine." Mel wiped her face with the back of her hand. "So, you broke my barn, did you?" he snarled at Nick.

"I didn't have a choice," Nick flustered. Freddy looked him up and down but Nick didn't care anymore. He looked at Mel, tucked firmly under her father's arm.

"Mel, why did you go? I have been so worried about you." "She's not your concern," Freddy replied with authority, moving Mel behind him protectively.

"I'm so sorry," Mel stuttered. "I can't...you don't understand," she began to sob again.

"I understand more than you think. Mel, people talk!" Nick stood forward, squaring off to Freddy.

"What people?" Freddy roared so loudly Nick stepped back again, he ordered Mel to get inside.

"Please, Dad!" she cried out.

"IN!" he shouted. Mel dropped her head, giving Nick one last look, her eyes full of sorrow, she turned and walked to her room. Joe stepped in her way.

"No," he said simply. Mel looked up hopefully. "Freddy, come on, we are going inside, Mel needs to talk to Nick." He turned Mel round to face Freddy and Nick standing next to each other.

"Over my dead..." Freddy began, but Joe stood firm, crossing his arms.

"It's time, Fred, she's not a baby anymore and I trust this boy." Freddy's face began to turn red in anger.

"He's a ..." again, Joe stopped him.

"...lovely, kind, honest, caring, financially stable man. Any fool can see that he loves our little girl. Look at him, Fred, look in his eyes. Look at your daughter." Joe placed his hand on Freddy's shoulder. Freddy looked from Nick to Mel, and back again. Nick was no longer intimidated by Mel's father.

"I do, I love her more than anything," he confessed, watching the smile spread across Mel's face, he knew she loved him too.

"You have no idea what you're getting into," Freddy growled.

"Then let me find out," Nick demanded firmly. "I love her, I will do whatever it takes to be with her, WHATEVER IT TAKES!" he emphasised.

"Well..." Freddy began, but again Joe came to his rescue.

"FREDERICK MATHEWSON, GET IN THIS HOUSE NOW." Nick couldn't help grinning, sucking in his lips to restrain himself. He had never heard Joe speak like that before, and judging by the surprised look on Freddy's face, neither had he. He grunted something inaudible and stormed into the house. "It's OK, Mel." Joe spoke softly to his daughter, "talk to him" he nodded towards Nick "..and see to his shoulder, it's bleeding quite badly and will get infected if you don't clean it up." He smiled a reassuring smile and followed Freddy into the house. The shouting that followed could be heard outside right across the yard.

"So?" Nick asked

"You really love me?" Mel replied. Nick strode across the yard and took her in his arms.

"If you never tell me, I will still love you with my entire soul. I knew the minute you touched my hand when we saw that amazing rainbow that I had fallen in love, that you were the one I wanted. I have felt so lost lately; all the fame and attention, it has just made me feel so lonely. Then I came here and I met you and everything changed. You made me feel confident again, in myself and my work. I need you," he assured her, then in the middle of the yard he kissed her, desperately needing the connection he could get from just holding her.

Mel cleaned up Nick's shoulder and dressed it, then sat on the corner of her bed biting her finger nails nervously; she had no idea where to begin. Nick waited patiently, he didn't want to rush her, she needed to tell him in her own time. She reached under her bed and pulled out a large, leather-bound book and handed it to him. He opened up the cover to see it was a sketch pad, each page contained drawings of everyone he had seen in the village, even Julian and Nell were in there.

"This is my family," Mel began, "everyone who has ever looked after me or helped raise me or just offered me a bed is in this book." Nick turned each

page then stopped when he saw a
face he recognised.

"You sketched me?" he asked, the drawing was
beautiful she had drawn him by the side of the
waterfall the day they had gone for a picnic, but the
way she had drawn him was breathtaking. Was this
how she saw him, he wondered? He looked so happy
and she had drawn an almost glow around him as he
ate the picnic, staring out at the waterfall. Mel
shrugged her shoulders and shyly looked down at
the floor, as he continued to turn the pages of the
book that was Mel's life. Every now and again there
was a picture of a dead tree or winter tree, stripped
of all its leaves and blossoms, it was a black
skeleton. When he asked her about it, she explained
that as a child she had quite a temper, so Joe told
her, anyway. She would fight against them and want
to run away and have a life with a name she could
tell everyone. When her temper would flare up Joe
used to make her draw this tree, then sit back and
imagine it blossoming, one by one she had to see
each blossom opening, if she lost concentration for
one minute she would have to start again. By the
time she had finished imagining blossom on every
branch she would forget what it was she was angry
about.

"That's genius," Nick commended. Mel smiled
sadly and began her story, or everything that she
knew about it at least.

Joe and Freddy had been out checking the beasts
around the farm, when they had come across a car

in the ditch, the woman inside was in labour. She refused to let them get help and so they delivered the baby as best as they could, using the little knowledge of animal husbandry that they had between them. The woman had been severely beaten, Joe could tell that much, also she was bleeding badly. Before she died she begged the men to take in her baby, she told them that she had got involved with a criminal, believing he would love her and take care of her. He had shown his true colours as soon as they had slept together; she had thought that he loved her, not realising that he was just using her for his own pleasure. Frightened, she had tried to run away but he had found her and threatened to give her to his men if she didn't co-operate and do exactly what he wanted her to do. Then he had unknowingly got her pregnant and when he discovered this, he had tried to kill her. However, she was smart, she had gathered evidence against him to protect herself but he was still hunting her. The woman had told Joe and Freddy that they were to hide the baby, tell no one and they were to get rid of her own body. She told them that the men might still come looking for her, for the baby, and kill her, she pleaded until they agreed to help.

"Freddy says that I had bright hair when I was born, caramel-coloured so they called me Mel," she stated matter of fact.

"You don't know your surname?" Nick exclaimed

"Don't know anything, everyone thought it best that the less we all knew the safer I would be."

The villagers all agreed to keep her safe, Freddy and Joe had driven the woman's car a few villages away then dumped it in the lake. A few years later it had been discovered by some divers, the police figured that the woman had just lost control of the car but as soon as the men found out who the body belonged to they came back to search for the woman's child. They visited and searched around each village every few years, following up leads or just hoping to randomly find the missing baby that was now a young adult.

"I guess he thinks my mother passed on some evidence or something, I don't know," Mel sighed sadly. Nick pulled her into his arms.

"I'm so sorry, Mel."

Mel was not sorry; she had had a wonderful life with many loving parents, although Freddy and Joe would always be her dads. At first she had lived with Joe and Freddy, they had raised her but when the men turned up the first time they got scared and so the village took it in turns. Some days she would stay with Rose and Alice, sometimes the Drake family, sometimes Joe and Freddy's. She learnt to travel light and so always carried spare clothes with her wherever she went, just in case.

"Still do that now," she amended pointing to her little rucksack,

"So you have no ID? No birth certificate, no driving licence?" Nick asked, astounded that someone could survive like that. "Hey, you drove my car with no licence," he suddenly remembered.

"Bigger picture, Nick!" she joked.

Mel had attended school but on the quiet, she did exams and tests, they were just never handed in, instead they were marked by the teachers and she was given a grade. As only so many exam papers were handed out, she completed an exam from the year before.

"I never saw the point in it when I was young, I mean I couldn't have any certificates to prove to anyone my exam results, so what was the point?" she told him. "But Joe would have blown his top if I didn't work hard, so I did it for him. I'm glad now, of course".

Mel worked wherever people needed help, if she was staying at someone's house then she would cook them a meal, if she needed some new clothes then she would work in the store or help out in the café, Rose and Alice were always good for material so Mel could make clothes herself.

"So when did all the tattoos start?" Nick asked. "Can't see your dads being happy about that." Mel laughed.

"No, not happy would be a major understatement. but I talk a good fight and they caved eventually. I stand out, you see, and if you were looking for someone in hiding you wouldn't even think twice about it being someone that stands out, would you?" she explained, proud of her theory.

"Yeah, I suppose so," he agreed, remembering how easily the men had accepted their story.

"So what if you want a loan?" he asked

"What for? I have a room, Dad made me that, I don't need to go on holiday, I mean, you have seen it around here!" Nick had to agree,

"OK, what about if you want to open a bank account?"

"I give my money to Freddy, it's safer than the bank, no one messes with Fred!"

"What about a library card?" Nick asked, thinking he had her but she just shrugged.

"I ask around the village, if someone has a book I want to read then I go spend a few days with them. I get to read the book; they get some needed chores done. I might just do some chores for money then Joe orders stuff for me online. There is always work that needs doing in the country and most of it is all seasonal, so cash in hand." She had an answer for everything, was it possible that someone could live completely off the grid?

"What about a wedding? You can never get married if you have no identity," he muttered solemnly, as the dreams he had for the two of them suddenly vanished into thin air. Mel's eyes began to swim with tears.

"No, that is the one thing I can never have, a forever."

Nick bit back the tears pooling in his eyes, his dreams of marrying Mel, of buying a house together, of doing all the normal couple things had, just vanished right before him. He was so close, so close to having the life he always wanted.

"It's OK, Nick." Mel spoke after a long silence, she could not bear to look him in the face. "It was always a dream, I will not blame you for leaving. You deserve a life with someone who can give you all the things you want."

Nick grabbed her face a little too roughly, disgusted with his selfishness. "Mel, I need you, just you. I may not be able to have all the things I want to with you, but I will have everything I need. No one will ever fill my heart like you do, I cannot offer you a forever, Mel, but I can offer you my heart, completely and honestly. I love you."

Mel looked up, tears finally falling, a relief like she had never known flowing through her. "You would stay? After everything that has happened? After everything I have told you?" Her voice crackled as she fought to control the emotion bubbling inside of her. Nick smiled and pressed his lips firmly to hers, pouring all the love he felt into her, proving his intent and determination.

"I want to stay with you forever."

Chapter 14

IT HAD BEEN three days since Mel's confession, and Nick had not left her side for a single second since then. He had stayed with her on the first night. Stayed in her tiny little room where she felt safe, held her through the night, comforted her, assuring her that it was his job now to look after her, it was where he belonged and if Mel let him it was where he would stay. He asked her to pack a few things and stay with him for a short while, no pressure, just a visit like she did with the other families in the village. Like a timid, wild animal, she was hesitant, to say the least.

"Look, I am in your book, am I not? You put me in your sketch book, that means I'm family now, right?" She reluctantly had to agree. "So you are just visiting like you do with all your family."

"Fine," she finally agreed "...but you can tell Freddy." Nick swallowed hard.

"Fine," he replied, suddenly not feeling as confident as he sounded.

"Fine, go on then he's outside." Nick had also heard his out of tune whistling.

Freddy had been less opposed to the idea than he thought, Joe it seemed had 'had words', and so when he told him about wanting Mel to stay with him for a while, he had just grunted and told him to make sure she kept in touch. Now Mel was in his house, in his bed and he was practically walking on air in delight and very determined to keep her there. He loved finding her clothes draped over everything, finding her makeup actually spread out on his sink and not in her little rucksack. Everywhere he looked Mel had made herself at home, spreading herself into every nook and cranny. Nick had even found her stuff in his wash bin mixed with his own, and somehow managed to find something strangely erotic and pleasing about the clothes entwined together in the same bin. He had become a little puppy following her everywhere, even to work.

"You don't have to stay here my whole shift, Nick," Mel complained as she served drinks in the pub. Nick sat at the bar reading his papers, drinking orange juice from the bottle, not that he didn't trust Mel, but after last time...

"Erm, that's my fault," Nell intervened. "I asked him to help lock up later, Julian's off on one of his day trips today and won't be back till late. Didn't I ask you ages ago, Nick?" Nell winked at him.

"Yeah, ages ago," he reiterated. "She asked me to stop behind ages ago." Mel just rolled her eyes at their little, wooden performance and muttered about feeling smothered. Nell offered him a high five and went off to serve another customer. Mel was right though, he couldn't follow her around forever, and the last thing he needed was her to bolt because she felt smothered. "Look," he called out to Mel.

"Nell doesn't need me till lock up
time, why don't I just pop home, do a bit of writing
and then come back to help lock up and walk home
with you?" He raised his eyebrows hopefully. Mel
just shook her head.

"Whatever," she said sarcastically. "It's not like
you won't fall asleep anyway!"

"I won't, I promise I will be here."

The familiar pain of keys stuck in his forehead
woke him from his sleep. "Oh damn," he uttered as
he peeled his face from the computer, what was it
with him dropping off to sleep lately? He should
have brought his laptop with him but George had
insisted he leave it and use the computer in the
cottage, he told him it would add to the experience.
"Fresh machine, fresh ideas," he had said
exuberantly. Nick tried to focus and looked at the
time on his screen. "Arrggh," he called out, as he
realised it was gone one o'clock in the morning.

"Arrgghh indeed," Mel repeated, with the same
sarcasm she had displayed in the pub.

"Baby, I am so sorry," he mumbled regretfully,
Mel just laughed.

"I can take care of myself, thank you, it's lovely
that you care but I am fine. I locked up with Nell and
she dropped me off in the car, so all is OK with the
world." She reached over and rubbed his head,
trying to remove the red imprint of the keys.

"It's better than OK," he corrected, gazing up into her eyes, "You hungry?" he asked.

"Already ate at the pub," she answered.

"Thirsty?"

"Duh, working in a pub!"

"Mmm," he pondered playfully. "What else do I have that you could possible want?" Mel moved slowly to stand in front of him, and leant right down to whisper in his ear.

"I only want one thing from you tonight, Nick;" she paused to kiss his earlobe, his head falling backwards as he groaned loudly.

"And what would that be, I wonder?" he played along, she smiled seductively.

"Your bath!" she replied and ran off up the stairs, stripping her clothes off one by one as she ran giggling. Nick chased her, feeling like a kid again.

"Mmm, a bath at one in the morning is not what I had in mind," Nick complained, not really meaning it. Nick was behind Mel, his arms wrapped tightly around her, holding her breasts whilst she lay with her back on his chest.

"Stop moaning, after a long shift this is heaven, Sundays are always a nightmare," she murmured, shifting to get more comfortable. "Nicholas!" she exclaimed and she felt his growing erection pressing into her back. "Good grief, a slight gust of wind will get you going!"

Nick chuckled. ."Not my fault," he defended "You moved and everything....jiggled!"

"God, you're like a randy teenager," Mel complained stepping out of the bath and wrapping a towel around herself, smacking him on the arm as she passed. Nick leant over the bath watching her as she got dry, grinning happily. He didn't care about her past, he didn't care that legally she didn't exist, he just cared about her and their future together. Surely they had one, you couldn't feel this strongly about someone and it not be the real deal. He loved her and wanted to shout it out, it didn't matter that he could never marry her, he could be content like this, living together happily. He wanted to give her the forever she dreamed of.

"Are you staying in there all night?" she asked, lying on the bed.

"Technically it's morning!" he corrected, "but yeah, the water is getting a bit cold."

Mel licked her lips as he got out of the bath, drying himself and draining the water. "Come here," she commanded curling her finger towards herself. As he neared the bed she lay on her stomach and reached for his still evident excitement. Nick backed off.

"Don't do that," he asked uncomfortably

"Why? What's the matter?" Mel asked and was slightly hurt, she never had a guy turn down that act before. Nick frowned.

"It's embarrassing," he looked everywhere but at Mel. "I had a girl do it once and she...well she... was kind of sick!" Mel spat out a laugh, then covered her mouth.

"I'm sorry, Nick, that must have been awful." She tried to sound genuine but the giggling wouldn't stop. Nick chewed his bottom lip.

"Well that's nice, Mel, one of the most horrendous moments of my life and you're laughing at me!" He was pissed, she could tell. Mel tried to regain herself.

"I'm sorry, it's just, well. She can't have been doing it properly, I mean it's just not something that should happen, Nick." She tried to calm herself, she slowed her breathing, desperately trying not to laugh again but her voice did nothing to disguise it.

"Maybe it was my size," Nick said, straight faced, this earned another snort from Mel.

"Yeah, of course that would be it," she responded condescendingly. Nick began to pout, he did not like this conversation at all and definitely did not like the attitude Mel was displaying right now. "Look, why don't you let me try, I promise I won't choke and promise that you will love it. Please Nick, let me try." His face was worried and he shook his head, the competition just turned Mel on more and she was determined to win. "Look, I will lie like this," she turned over so that she was lying on her back and shuffled so that her head was hanging slightly off the edge. "See," she stroked her throat. "Like a sword swallower, in this position my neck and throat are aligned so nothing to get in the way, my gag reflex will be lessened!"

Nick was losing the battle, Mel was lying in front of him, her towel had undone and was now beneath her. She laid on her back, her breasts jutting up to the ceiling, completely naked and his imagination began to run riot. It's true in this position he could just step back if he wasn't happy, he would be in complete control at all times. Slowly he stepped forward. Mel grinned satisfactorily, she was winning.

He stood before her, his erection poised at her lips, his eyes fixed upon her breasts as she breathed heavily. Slowly she smoothed her hands up the backs of his legs and round to his deliciously taut backside. Nick relaxed a little and took a tiny step forwards, Mel saw her opportunity; she grabbed his backside and pushed him into her mouth, all the way. He cried out and jumped back. "What the hell?" he cried out furiously. Mel just laughed.

"See, no choking," she cheered.

"That's not even funny, it's just...wrong. I can't believe you did that." He stormed over to the other side of the room.

"Look, Nick, I just needed to show you that I won't have a problem, you need to relax and you can now that you know I can do it. Why don't you come here and let me continue?" Nick was furious and paced up and down, what the hell was wrong with her? That was the most embarrassing moment he had ever experienced and she was just making fun of him, but the blood was rapidly leaving his brain and going into other areas, resulting in him struggling to focus. Mel lay down again. "Please, Nick," she put on a fake girly little voice and damn if it wasn't working on him. Panic flooded through him, it was true she hadn't choked or made any noise, maybe she was right, maybe he could just try it, just once. Every other man seemed to enjoy it; he had listened to all his uncles and their rude late night conversations. They said it was amazing, better than sex, although he found that very hard to believe, but Mel looked so beautiful, so desperate to make him happy.

"Slowly!" he instructed, the anger he had felt just a minute ago fading into excitement as he tiptoed back over to her. Mel crossed her fingers and made a cross sign over her heart. This was definitely a first for her, never had she had to convince a guy to let her pleasure him, and the challenge was turning her on fiercely. He moved to stand in front of her.

"Let's give you something else to concentrate on, shall we?" she suggested and taking his hands placed them over her breasts, knowing it would render him powerless. Nick was definitely infatuated with her breasts and he growled his approval. Who knew he was a breast man? He'd never really been that bothered before, but Mel's, he couldn't leave alone. Pulling him into her she began again, slowly this time. She flicked the tip with her tongue, causing him to inhale sharply, her hand reached down and her nails gently scratched his base. Nick's mind disintegrated, it felt so good, then Mel kissed and licked the underside of his throbbing erection, taking only his tip into her mouth then pulling back. Unconsciously Nick found himself pushing forward, wanting more, needing her to take him all. She took the hint, sucking in her lips she slowly took him all the way to the back of her throat.

"Oh my God," he called out in ecstasy at the new sensation, how had he not noticed the tongue piercing before that now massaged the top of him whilst her hand grazed and caressed his balls? He wasn't going to last that was for sure, this was mind-blowing, he had never ever felt anything so good. He wanted it to last but at the same time he needed release and began quickening his pace. Realising where his hands were he began to play, gently stroking her breasts, catching her between his fingers and pulling slightly. Mel arched up off the bed and hummed in appreciation and it sent him over the edge, the vibrations from her sound ricocheted through every part of him and he could stand it no longer. He tried to pull back but Mel held him tightly in place, refusing to release him. He called out her name and cursed as he found release, his legs shaking as she continued to caress him.

"Well?" she asked, sitting up and licking her lips, Nick leaned on the bed in the same position but leaning forward onto his hands. "Nick?" Mel asked again, his silence concerned her, she worried she had caught him with her tongue piercing, wouldn't be the first time. Maybe he needed his inhaler, crap, she hadn't thought about that. Nick slowly looked into her eyes, speechless. He turned and collapsed onto the floor, leaning his back up against the bed, taking a long deep breath. Realising that he was OK and not, as she thought, having an asthma attack, Mel moved onto her stomach to gently kiss his shoulders, running her nails through his hair. "Are you OK, sweetheart?" Nick held up his finger.

"You, wow...I mean...wow." Mel grinned, yes she had done well. "You..." he repeated over and over again "...I will deal with in a minute!" he threatened.

"You dealt with me the other night," she giggled "it was your turn."

"Oh no, oh no," he protested "That was... that was...I need a drink." Mel walked over to the bathroom area where there was a glass that she could fill with water. She strutted, still naked, over to him and handed him his drink. Nick slowly sipped the water, waiting for his brain to refill with blood so that he could think straight. She was amazing, beautiful and clever and the way she made him feel, not just then but all the time...he was never going to let her go.

Nick turned to face the bed again where Mel was sitting in the middle of it again; tiny fireworks were still exploding in front of his eyes. "Your turn," he grinned goofily and grabbed her ankles, dragging her to the edge of the bed. Mel shrieked loudly laughing as he dragged her down the bed.

"Nick, stop it," she protested

"Never, never ever ever," he repeated, then smiled with satisfaction as her laughing stopped and turned to moans of pure pleasure.

Chapter 15

NICK LAY WATCHING the sun streaming in through the window, dust particles floated around inside each beam creating a sort of mist-like image. He turned to watch Mel sleep, it wasn't the first time that he had done that. Her face scrubbed of makeup and hair loose, she looked like a sleeping angel, her pale skin almost iridescent in the light. She moaned softly and snuggled her face deeper into her pillow. Nick smiled, so content to be here with her, he pushed a stray strand of hair from her face allowing him to see her better. Her eyelashes fluttered open.

"Mmm morning," she purred. "Oh my God, you're not watching me sleep are you?" she asked, embarrassed.

"Me? No course not," he lied. "Why would I want to listen to you snore? And watch you drool all over your pillow!" She pulled a face and stuck out her tongue, turning away from him. Nick laughed and pulled her back across the bed to him, he kissed the back of her neck and whispered,

"I love you Mel, so much. I don't know what I did to deserve this but I am so much in love," and cuddled her closer, slotting his body perfectly in behind her.

"I think I love you too," she admitted honestly.

"Think?" he shouted out outraged. "You think you do!" and with that he tickled her ribs, sending her into hysterical bursts of laughter. He loved her laugh, loud and unashamed she roared out, tears streaming down her face.

"Stop it, I can't breathe," she begged. Nick was interrupted by the phone.

"This isn't over," he promised and walked downstairs to grab it. Mel moved over to the bath, turning on the taps to fill the tub, she needed to calm down and try to get some sanity back.

"Nick, darling how are you? I haven't heard from you for over a week," his mother's voice crooned down the line.

"Mum, hey." He was delighted to hear her voice; he had missed her and had meant to check in to see that she was OK. "How's things going? Are you OK in the flat on your own?" he asked. There was a long pause on the phone.

"You're very ... animated this morning," she noted, Nick rolled his eyes. His mother should work for the government, she could sniff out a secret at one hundred paces. He took a deep breath.

"Mum, I've met someone, a girl, she's...she's different. But, Mum, I really like her, like really, really like her. I think this is serious and I know it's only been a week but..." he sighed. "I think I'm in

love, Mum." There was a sharp
intake of breath from the other side of the call, then
his mum spoke softly.

"Nick, different is good. Everyone said that your
dad was no good for me. They said actors will sleep
with all their leading ladies and that he would break
my heart. But we loved each other desperately and
were so happy together, I wouldn't change a single
moment of my time with your dad. Listen, Nick, your
dad and I and Uncle George raised a smart boy, if
you love her, then we will love her, sweetheart, trust
your instincts, if it feels right to you and not too
soon then it must be right. Just be careful, don't rush
things, love, and take your time. The beginning is
really the best part, don't miss it." Nick closed his
eyes, he shouldn't doubt his mother, he had worried
about what she might think about all the tattoos, but
she would love Mel, he just knew it.

"I love you, Mum."

"I love you too, sweetheart, now listen I know you
are having a break and I am glad it's working out
well but you need to give Melissa a call, she's
drowning in work here. I am sure she would
appreciate an appearance for a day or two." Nick
promised that he would call her straight away. With
the work part of the conversation over, which had
initially been the main reason his mother had called
him up, his mother wanted to hear all about Mel,
how they met? What she was like? What her family
were like? Nick obliged as much as he could without
revealing all Mel's secrets, not easily done with his

mother in full 'secret sniffing out' mode. His mother told him that she had been helping Uncle George out more and had been doing a little bit of work in the theatre again.

"That's great, Mum," Nick enthused; his mother had disappeared from the theatre since the death of his father, so hearing that she was working a little delighted him. He told his mum how proud he was of her; he could hear her sniffles as she said a quick goodbye to him, citing the reason that she had to dash off. He hung up and heaved a sigh, he heard Mel splashing about in the bath and so decided to give Melissa a quick call.

His mother was right, Melissa was working her backside off for him and he was hiding away, enjoying himself and shirking all his responsibilities. She told him all about the book sales and that the fuss over the radio interview had disappeared completely, no one had given it a second thought. Melissa laughed when she told him that someone else had done a kiss and tell story about the girl who had lied about him, told them that she had slept with loads of guys at school etc., after that no one had believed the story she had spun about Nick cheating on her. "It's ironic really," Melissa chuckled. That seemed a lifetime ago now, he had completely forgotten all about it but Melissa was still apologising.

"Melissa, please forget it, I was tired and stressed out and took it out on you, I'm the one who should be sorry. Look, how would it be if I came back for a

few days? I can sign all the
contracts, do a few interviews and just get up to date
with everything."

"Nick, that would be great," she gushed, relieved,
"a few days would make a huge difference, I mean it
is slowing down and we are getting to the point that
you can go off and do some writing but there are
still a few bits and pieces that need doing and just
finishing up." She paused before adding, "So you like
it up there then?" Nick smiled,

"Yeah, I like it a lot."

"Need any help?" he asked hopefully as he
ambled back into the bedroom. Mel handed him the
wash cloth and he happily obliged. "I have to go back
for a few days," he told her. The second his words
left his mouth he felt her tense up, her shoulders
raising and tightening. He dropped the wash cloth
and gentle kissed her neck. "Just a few days and then
I will be back, I promise." Mel nodded but stood up
abruptly and wrapped a towel tightly around her;
Nick felt the atmosphere change dramatically.
"Mel?"

"Look, it's fine," she answered sharply. "People
come and go all the time, people promise to come
back but they never do, so let's not pretend," she
barked, stand-off-ish. Nick was not going to let her
do this; she was not going to push him away.

"Mel, I know you have only dated tourists before
but I am not like them. This is a family home; I am

not just passing through. Mel, I want to make my life here...with you, I love you." He turned her to face him, wrapping his arms around her waist. "I love you," he reiterated, trying to convince her. She nodded, not entirely confident, she wanted to believe him, was desperate to believe him, but history told her she could not trust his words.

"The best things can't be planned, Nick, let's just see how it goes," and she grabbed her clothes and walked over to the sink to get ready. Nick sighed, what could he do to convince her? What could he say? He resigned himself to that fact that Mel was complicated, it would take a long time for her to trust him properly but that was OK, he was not one to shy away from a bit of hard work and by God, Mel was worth it.

It was suddenly awkward between the two as they ate their breakfast, Mel couldn't make eye contact with him and for the first time in his life he was struggling to find the words he wanted to say.

"So when will you leave?" she asked glumly.

"Today. Later this afternoon, I think, but it will only be a few days," he assured her again. Mel just nodded, placing another piece of scrambled egg into her mouth. "My mother wants to meet you," he blurted out. Mel looked at him with wide, petrified eyes,

"What?" she uttered through a mouthful of food. 'Ha, she hadn't expected that,' he thought.

"Well, it was her on the phone earlier and I told her all about you and she wants to meet the woman that's captured her son's heart," he smiled, reaching out to brush the rebellious strand of hair away from her eyes that were still startled.

"I... well...what if she doesn't like me?" she worried in a high pitched voice, the worry of him leaving now replaced with the worry of meeting his family.

"Impossible, she will love you, just like I do." He leaned over the table and placed a gentle, soft, chaste kiss on her forehead. Sitting back, he noticed her face had returned to normal and she was smiling sweetly.

"I love you, Nick" she declared. "I'm just...scared." He shook his head.

"I know, me too but it's OK."

The unnerving quiet returned and Nick found himself offering to help her find out why the men were hunting her. "I can do some searches whilst I am at the office," he suggested. "Look up old papers and that, what do you think?" Mel gazed at him hopefully; she had so little information about the woman that had given birth to her. She knew nothing about her family or what they were like; she did not even know her surname. As for the men that hunted her, they were looking for something, information, evidence, who knew, but Mel had nothing, her mother had nothing in her possession when she died, no ID hidden in the glove box, no purse or handbag, she had no identity, just like Mel.

"Do you think you could find anything out?" she asked hopefully.

"Can't do any harm trying." He stood to answer the phone that was ringing again.

"Nick-ol-arse?" the voice asked, no guesses as to who that was! "I need to talk to Mel." Nick handed the phone over.

"It's your father," he announced, rolling his eyes up to the ceiling, then moved into the garden to give her some privacy.

The garden was in full bloom, the height of summer had resulted in flowers of every colour and size erupting all over. It reminded him of the rainbow he had seen when walking with Mel. The amazing, full arch rainbow that had taken his breath away, just like Mel had. He smiled, this garden was Mel, it summed up everything he loved about her, the multi-coloured style, the wildness and beauty and the sense of calm he felt around her, that he felt now, this minute. As he looked out into the garden he didn't see the dead chickens strewn all over the grass or the blood streaks anymore, he saw peace. He saw home.

"Oh my gosh, Nick, Nick!" Mel called out and rushed into his arms. "Millie's coming home,

Freddy's going to pick her up and
the pups!" she screamed excitedly. "I'm so happy,
Nick, I thought I'd lost her." Tears fell as she circled
round and round him. "I couldn't bear to lose her."
Nick felt dizzy.

"Stop, stop, stand still," he laughed, "that's great, I
am so pleased." He sensed that there was a
connection with her and her dog. The look on Mel's
face as she saw the dog lying on the barn floor,
crying in pain, had almost destroyed Nick. Visions of
Mel's mother flooded his mind, of her begging Joe
and Freddy to take care of her baby then dying in
their arms. Is that what Mel saw? Why she had felt
unable to act? Emotion overwhelmed him and he
grabbed her close, hiding her from the tears that
threatened to fall.

"You saved her, you know," she whispered
against his chest. "I never thanked you for saving
her and the little runt." Nick guffawed.

"Freddy chucking it about saved the little one," he
corrected. "I was useless." Mel stepped back, wiping
the tears from her own eyes.

"No, if you hadn't found her..." she trailed off.

"I came for you," he told her. "I came to find you, I
just happened to hear Millie. I was lucky." Mel shook
her head once more.

"You always seem to appear at the moment I
need you, don't you. I needed someone to love in my

life and suddenly you turn up, Millie was dying and there you were again, just where I needed you to be. You really are for real, aren't you?" she said slowly, as though it was finally registering. Nick said nothing, just held her, a serene expression on his face as he accepted the fact that Mel was lowering her walls, allowing him past her defences and letting him love her.

The vet had told Freddy that they needed to keep the other animals away from Millie and her pups for a while, she was very delicate and the three older pups could worry her wounds. Mel had told him that she was going to keep them in her little flat so she could watch them all the time.

"Listen," Nick announced, suddenly having an idea. "Why don't you stay here?" Mel frowned but Nick pushed on regardless. "Look, I'm not going to be here for a few days anyway so you can have the place to yourself. The pups can have the run of the garden and Millie can relax and get better, my place is closer to the village so wherever you are working you can pop back easily to check on them." He could see that Mel was warming to the idea. "Don't forget, at yours the older pups are going to be barking outside and trying to get in through that flap on the door."

"I suppose that makes sense," she mused. Nick's heart did somersaults, he pushed on.

"Don't forget that Millie might need her wounds bathing, here you could run a shallow bath and bathe her." Mel's expression at this was priceless.

"You would let me bathe my dog in your posh bath?" she asked, not believing a word.

"I wouldn't be here to argue the fact," he reminded her. Mel grinned and after a lifetime of waiting she agreed to stay. Nick was ecstatic, she was moving in for a few days, true, he was not going to be here but still it was a big step.

"It's a good job it wasn't Fred that fell ill," she laughed at her own joke. Nick raised an eyebrow. "Oh, Fred's my other pet, the highland cow that you pass on the way into the village."

Nick's mouth fell open. "That beast is a pet!" he gasped, the monster that had stuck its head in his car when he first arrived was her pet! Mel giggled.

"Yeah, some farmer had him in with all his beasts, then just decided he didn't want him anymore so turned him loose, just like that, can you believe it? He's such a magnificent animal isn't he, I used to groom him when I was little, he loves a good bath but I don't think I could fit him in yours!" Mel talked on and on about this fierce creature with deadly horns like it was a kitten. "He is an acquired taste," she added, seeing the disbelief in Nick's eyes. "Are you sure this is OK?" she added, "me staying here?"

"Sure, it will be great, it's a perfect solution. I will leave you my key and that way you have to be here when I get back to let me in," he beamed.

"Mmm, that's sneaky, Mr Mill-Thorpe." Mel narrowed her eyes "Trying to trap me here, are you?" she said amused, secretly delighted that he was definitely coming back.

"Trap is a bit harsh." He pretended to be hurt, Mel stood up onto her tiptoes and kissed the end of his nose.

"Oh right then," she rephrased. "Make sure I stay with you."

"Forever," he insisted, and kissed her without waiting for a reply.

Chapter 16

NICK SAT FIDGETING, not really listening to what was being said in the meeting, it was Saturday morning and he had been away from Mel for nearly five days. He had tried to call every day but Mel's life was full, she had answered once but every other time the phone had just rung. He imagined her out in the garden playing with her dog Millie or cuddling up into bed with all the puppies around her. He knew that's what was happening, Mel loved her animals and there was no way she would have Millie and her puppies sleep downstairs, they would be in bed with her, probably snuggled up on his pillow, taking his place!

"Something amusing?" Melissa asked, irritated.

"Sorry," Nick apologised. "I am happy with whatever Melissa thinks is best," he added, smiling at his agent.

"Really?" she asked, shocked at his sudden compliance, Nick usually fought her on most of her plans or ideas, he was acting very strangely.

"Look, Melissa, you have looked after me from the very start, I know that and I know you will do what is best for me. So long as I am not away from home for long periods then I am on board with whatever you say," he said earnestly. Melissa eyed him warily.

"OK, OK," she accepted. "But which home are we talking about?" She had a smug look on her face that told him his mother had been talking; he just smiled and ignored her.

The meeting went on for another hour about marketing, budgets etc etc. Melissa had hired a team to deal with all Nick's fan mail so that only genuine letters would be passed onto him, no more knickers in the post! Nick sat back gratefully; Melissa had really come up trumps, she was a real-life diamond and he now realised how much she actually did for him. Every aspect of his life was now scheduled and organised, and he knew well in advance everything he was doing or anything he had been invited to do. Melissa had been able to ensure that he would never be away from home longer than two weeks in any one period without having a week or two off in-between. Perfect.

They had been tied up in the meeting since eight o clock in the morning but as eager as he was to return to Mel he wanted to thank Melissa properly; dashing out to a nearby florists he chose the biggest bouquet he could find. It was full of roses, daisies, carnations and ferns. It was a rainbow of colours and would brighten her office up greatly. As Nick walked through the office the girls all let out little sighs and noises, Melissa stood to greet him.

"What are you doing here? I thought you would be on the motorway by now," she said, dragging him into an obligatory cuddle.

"I wanted to give you these." He handed over the flowers as Melissa frowned, not understanding. "I don't say thank you half as much as I should and I need you to know I do appreciate it. Everything you do, Melissa, I am so grateful to you and I promise no more fights," he grinned his charming grin. "Or temper tantrums either." Melissa melted, shaking her head.

"You are my most challenging client, you know that don't you, Nick," she informed him. "Most people would kill to be famous, do anything I ask them to do and then some, I can't get them enough interviews, but you... you want anonymity but you want to be successful." She let out a long hard sigh. "You cannot have one without the other, Nick, I wish you could. If I could arrange it for you I would do it but..." she drifted off.

"No more, whatever you tell me to do I will do. As long as I get free time I will follow your lead," he promised.

"Wow, she must be special." Melissa looked at the beautiful flowers.

"I knew my mother had been talking," he muttered grumpily, Melissa laughed.

"Talking! She has been screaming it from the rooftops, got you married off and picking out names for her grandchildren," she giggled. "Nick, have I said something wrong?" she asked seeing his face twist and contort as though in pain. He shook his head forcing a smile, he would never be able to give his mother the wedding she wanted, she would never see her son married off to a lovely girl. He wanted that so much but as far as the law was concerned Mel didn't exist, there was nothing he could do about that. If he could suddenly create an identity for her so she could be legal, he would. He had hoped that his searches on the internet would help, that he would be able to link Mel to her mother and therefore give her a surname, but all his efforts had failed. He could find no records to say the woman dragged from the lake had ever had a child, and no leads to follow to find out who exactly was hunting Mel down.

Melissa looked at the sadness on his face, but before she could ask him about it a disturbance in the office distracted her.

"What's going on?" she asked, as she ran over to where the huddle of women all talked loudly and at once.

"It's Cam," they managed. Nick looked at the girl sobbing as she sat at her desk, her face was bright red on one side, a handprint clearly becoming visible.

"Alright, girls, why don't you back up a minute and give her some space," Nick suggested. "Cam, isn't it?" he asked, the girl nodded in between sobs. "Why don't we go into Melissa's office, and could someone get a coffee or tea please?" One of the other

office women agreed, and headed
towards the kitchen. Melissa looked at Nick as they
led her to the office, her eyes full of fear. "OK, Cam,
why don't you tell us exactly what has happened, in
your own time and we can try to help." The girl
accepted the tissue that Melissa handed her and
tried to calm herself a little to enable her to speak.
She explained that she had been going out to lunch,
to meet a man she had started seeing, they had been
on one date that had gone really well and now he
wanted to meet her for lunch.

"It started off really good," she whimpered. "He
had bought me flowers and we talked about a film I
wanted to see. Then he ... tried to kiss me." The tears
began again as she spoke, but neither Nick nor
Melissa interrupted her. "I wasn't ready for it, you
see, I didn't expect him to kiss me and it caught me
off guard." A feeling of dread began to brew up in
Nick's stomach, he glanced over to Melissa and saw
that she too had the same sense and had begun to
write down exactly what Cam was telling them.

"Go on," he encouraged her, speaking as softly as
he could.

"I pulled back, you see," she said guiltily. "It was
just a reaction, I didn't mean anything by it. He just
snapped, changed just like that," she snapped her
fingers and began staring at the floor. "He called me
every name under the sun, said I had been teasing
him, leading him on. He really scared me..." she
looked up at Nick for reassurance.

"Of course you would be scared," Melissa said, outraged, but Nick silenced her with his hand.

"Go on, Cam, what did he do?" Not that Nick wanted to find out what that man had done to her but he knew she had to get all the facts out now whilst they were fresh in her mind. He knew Melissa was writing everything down so he prepared himself for the worst and encouraged her to continue.

"I tried to leave, but he grabbed me." She lifted up the sleeves of her shirt to reveal large bruises that were forming on her upper arms. Melissa let out a little gasp. "I kicked him, between the legs. I just reacted." She was speaking fast now, her words tripping over themselves as they tumbled from her mouth. "He slapped me round the face and I fell into the next table. That's when the manager came over and made him leave."

"We need to call the police," Melissa stated.

"No, no," Cam panicked. "Please, I don't want them involved." Nick leant over and took Cam's hands into his own.

"Cam, I know you are scared but this bloke needs dealing with, he hurt you, he could have hurt other woman like you. They need to know about this." He assured her that he would stay with her until they came but it was her decision, eventually she agreed to call them.

The police arrived shortly after Melissa placed the call, they took Cam's statement and although they could not guarantee what action would be taken, they did assure her that she had done the right thing and agreed that none of it had been her fault. They had given her a contact number should this man ever turn up again, and she felt a little more secure knowing that they had taken her seriously and intended to call again in a week or so to make sure she was OK. Melissa suspected that the young officer had in fact taken a shine to Cam and that was the reason he was offering her a re-visit, but nevertheless Cam was beginning to stop crying. Nick and Melissa drove Cam home and offered to stay.

"Please, I am fine now, I promise, you have too much work to do, I am sorry for causing all this fuss," she flustered with her keys. Nick took them from her.

"No fuss, you have had a horrible experience and everyone is here for you, Cam." He opened the door wide to allow her to walk in.

"Now lock the door and call me if there are any concerns or if you just want to talk, OK?" Melissa instructed and they left Cam after hearing that she had locked the door behind them.

"I can't believe that," Melissa said, shocked as they returned to the office. "That poor girl." Nick agreed, he never understood violence. He had been brought up in a loving home and had never received so much as a smack off his parents. He could not understand how anger could transgress into violence, how you could possibly hurt another human being.

"Oh, Nick, it is nearly past one o'clock. Aren't you supposed to be in the village by now?" It was true but he had to make sure Cam was OK first; he kissed Melissa on the cheek and made his way to the car. He couldn't wait to see Mel, he needed to hold her in his arms and know that she was OK. Poor Cam had no one to look after her and it made him feel bad but at least he could love Mel. So what if they couldn't marry? Being with someone he loved so much would be enough for him.

Nick wound his window down and shouted out a mighty 'hello' to Fred as he passed him, Fred mooed loudly in response and Nick laughed, he was going to see Mel in a matter of minutes and his heart was already racing. He pulled up to the pub as he presumed she would be there, if not it was as good a place as any to start, tracking someone down who didn't have a phone was not easy.

"Nick," Nell hollered as he walked through the doors. "How are you, dear? It's so good to see you again." She dashed from around the bar and hugged him tightly. Nick returned her embrace.

"Is she here?" he asked, not needing to state whom.

"Not yet," Nell replied. "In fact she's quite late, she said she would be here at about two but it's nearly three now." Nick felt bile rise up from his stomach. Mel was erratic, that was true, but if she gave someone a time then she would be there.

"Do you know where she was this morning?" he asked, trying to remain calm.

"Yes, she was at the shop, I will ring Mr Michaels now, find out what's happening, he's probably got her stacking peas!" she joked, but after a long wait there was no reply and Nell's face began to show the worry. "There's no reply," she stated in a panicked voice. "Mr Michaels never shuts the shop early, never!" Nick didn't hesitate, he turned heels and ran not even collecting his car, he just ran. Something was wrong, he could feel it, something had happened to her.

Mr Michael's shop came into view and he fought to keep his legs running and his breath calm, as he reached the shop Joe and Freddy pulled up in their truck. Nell had called them and the two fathers had a wild, fierce predatory look on their faces now. Nick reached the door first; the shop appeared to be empty.

"Mr Michaels!" Nick called out, "Are you here? Mel? Mr Michaels?" There was a groan from behind the counter and Freddy leapt over it in one single bound. Mr Michaels lay on the floor, his head bleeding, his lip swollen.

"Where's Mel?" Freddy demanded, but Mr Michaels shook his head.

"They took her," he murmured weakly. "There were two henchmen and one big guy, the boss, I think." He coughed as he tried to sit up. Nell came running in behind them and let out a scream as she saw the blood.

"Call Bill," Joe instructed. "He's the paramedic on duty this week, he will call an ambulance but you will need him here first, the ambulance will take too long." Nell nodded and ran outside to make the call. Joe turned again. "I know it's hard but what happened? Do you know where they took her?" he asked hopefully. Mr Michaels swallowed and tried to clear his throat.

"They came in and locked the door behind them, they asked questions about Mel, whether she had been researching her mother." He coughed, and blood came out of his mouth. Joe gently wiped it away. "They laughed then grabbed her, told her she couldn't escape and asked her if she had something that didn't belong to her. Asked her if she had a safe but Mel wasn't having any of it, just told them to get lost and tried to get away from them. They joked about something, something about taking a long fall and that she would tell them what they wanted to know when she was up there, that's all I know." Joe nodded gratefully and glanced sideways, indicating that the men should step outside. Nick's world collapsed, where was she? Had they hurt her? He needed to find her and set off frantically looking

around for a sign, anything that
might indicate which direction they took.

"Nick! Nick, wait," Joe called out, he turned to
Freddy. "We need to think, if we rush off we may
never find her. Listen, they said taking a fall, that
means somewhere high up, where could they have
meant?" Freddy raised his hands, clueless.

"Everywhere is high round here," he snapped.

"Wait." Nick thought. "They have to come into the
village the same way, yes? It's on a horseshoe shape,
the whole village, same way in and out." Both men
agreed. "Then they would have to come over the
stone bridge, it's not that high but a fall off it..." He
didn't need to finish his sentence, Joe and Freddy
leapt into action, jumping into the truck. Nick didn't
wait for an invitation and threw himself into the
back. Freddy sped off, spinning the wheels as he
rushed towards the bridge, gravel shooting out from
the tyres, spraying the shop front. "Please, God, let
us be in time," Nick prayed, he was not a violent man
but he would protect Mel with his life.

Freddy saw the car first, parked on the side of the
road, the bridge just up ahead. He pointed to Joe.
"You go across the river and come up on the other
side." Joe nodded and headed off. He then turned to
Nick. "You take this." He reached into the back of the
truck and pulled out a rifle. "You ever fired one?"
Nick shook his head. Freddy showed him how to
crack the gun and reload, then how to aim and fire.
Looking down the barrel of the gun, he practised

lining up the sight to show where he wanted to shoot, it was frightening but he was willing, he was prepared to do whatever it took to get Mel back. All those times he had seen soldiers in the village, all the stories Rose and Mel had told him, and today, when he could have really used them, there was not a soldier in sight. Freddy was heading straight towards the bridge; Nick was to go down to the river's edge to see if he could get a shot. "That's my baby girl in danger, Nick!" Freddy's voice wavered as he spoke; Nick nodded, needing no further incentives and headed down the stream, wading ankle deep through the water.

Moving as quietly as he could he skirted around some of the bushes and trees that edged and overhung the river. It was then he saw her, her hair now a shocking red colour, she was on the bridge, three men surrounding her, he strained to hear what was being said and raised up the rifle to get a better look through the sight.

"Quite a view up here, isn't it?" the large fat man observed, the two henchmen agreed.

"Yeah, lovely, boss!"

"Yeah, a real picture."

"I can see why you live here." The large fat man stroked a finger down Mel's cheek, Mel turned and spat hard into his face; he grimaced then reached back and slapped her across the face, sending her flying into the low wall along the edge. They had

walked her up to the middle of the
bridge that crossed a shallow river, the entrance
that took you into the village itself. She had fought
them at first but when they had beaten Mr. Michaels
she had agreed to go with them, calmly. Terrified
that they would kill him, she thought if she could get
them away from the shop then she might stand a
chance of escaping. The fat man dragged her up by
her hair.

"So you are my long lost daughter, are you?" he
sneered. "I believe you have something that belongs
to me, something your mother left you?" Mel tried
her best to look confused.

"I don't know what you're talking about!" she
cried. "My mother is at home with my brother and
sister." Another slap landed on her other cheek, her
face now on fire, but she refused to cry out, refused
to give him the satisfaction of knowing he had hurt
her, of knowing that right now she was scared,
frightened that she was going to die, die alone just
like her mother. Nick saw Freddy lurch forward the
moment his little girl got hurt, a murderous
expression on his face. Joe was on the other side of
the bridge and furiously waved at him to stop,
indicating that he should wait, they couldn't get to
the henchmen without Mel getting in the way. Nick
fought the fear that was causing his chest to
constrict, making him wheeze, and familiar black
spots darted around his vision. Swallowing hard, he
attempted to regulate his breathing, telling himself
over and over again that he could not fall apart now,
Mel needed him.

"Don't lie, little girl, someone has been researching, do you think I wouldn't have any web sites linked to that bitch's death monitored?" Nick's heart stopped beating, it was his fault, and he had done an internet search on all the newspaper reports he could find that mentioned the woman in the lake, curious to find out what had happened, to help Mel. But his meddling had put her in danger, if she got hurt, it would be his entire fault.

"You are a lying bitch, just like your tart of a mother, she begged me, you know, begged me to give her a new life, to fuck her!" The fat man roared with laughter as Mel threw herself at him, fists flying wildly.

"Bastard!" she spat out as she tried to kick and punch the man. He grabbed her wrists and easily held her firm, laughing at her futile attempts.

"You definitely have her spirit." He pulled her close to whisper in her ear, "...but you have my temper, sweetheart." A tear fell from Mel's eye as the realisation sunk in, this was her father, she was a part of this monster.

"Tell me about her," she managed to utter as she swallowed the bile that was rising in her throat.

"Your mother? Well, where to start?" The fat man threw her against the side of the bridge, hard, and Mel collapsed to her knees. "She was a little girl when I found her, but I taught her to be a woman, ripped the virginity from her." This caused the two henchmen to smirk and laugh at Mel's shocked expression. "I offered to share her with my men but she only wanted me!" He looked down at her. "Maybe you don't want to hear about this, little girl, maybe you don't want to hear about how I raped her, beat her and then when I was done - I ordered her disposed of!" Mel let out a loud sob, her poor, poor mother. What sort of life did she live to think that this demon could offer her something better? He was right, she did not want to know, all she needed to know was that her mother had protected her, at the very end she had given up her own life to save her daughter's, and she would always love her even though she knew nothing about her. Mel slowly staggered to her feet.

"I don't give a shit what you say to me, my mother got the better of you, didn't she, I mean she was nothing to you but she protected herself and now... now she is everything to you, isn't she?" A satisfied smile erupted from Mel as she saw the fat man's face begin to turn a bright shade of purple. She was getting to him. "So tell me, how exactly did this insignificant young girl manage to steal something so important?" She had no idea what exactly her mother did take from this man but it must be important if he was willing to spent years searching for it. She wished her mother had left her something, then maybe she could have helped to put this sick bastard away. She had gathered from what he was telling her and from what Joe and Freddy had told her, this man had basically murdered her mother. The beating she had received had killed her and nearly killed Mel, she would have given anything to have her revenge and see him behind bars.

The fat man walked over to Mel and grabbed her by the throat; she gasped, fighting for air, as his fingers closed tighter around her throat. "Do you really think that I would not do to you exactly what I did to your mother? First, little girl, I would take you, I would cause you pain as I took my revenge out on you, then I would hand you over to my boys and they would take turns with you and by the time they had all finished there would be nothing left and I would discard you like I did your slut of a mother!" He released his grip only for a second to allow him to punch her straight in the jaw. She cried out and fell to the ground, blood seeping from her lip. A rustling sound had the two men raising their guns; they looked at the fat man, who raised his head giving the signal that they should investigate. Both men headed in opposite directions searching for the origin of the sounds.

Nick wiped the tears from his eyes as he tried to focus, Mel was hurt, they were punching her and he could not do anything about it. He raised the rifle again but just couldn't get a clean shot, Mel had been dragged to her feet again and any attempt to hit the fat man would result in him hitting Mel. With a suddenly flood of delight he saw Joe and Freddy emerge at either ends of the bridge, the men dealt with; they now pointed the confiscated guns at the fat man who was holding their daughter. The man spun around quickly so that Mel was shielding him and held a previously secreted knife to her throat.

"One more step, lads," he warned, both men froze but did not lower their guns. Nick now had a clean shot of the man's back but didn't dare take it with the knife at Mel's throat. His heart pounded as he watched the standoff, sweat pouring from his brow as he waited, waited for his chance.

"She doesn't know anything," Joe shouted. "Her mother left nothing with her; she is of no use to you!" The fat man smiled.

"Well, thanks for clearing that up for me," he smirked. "Now I have no reason to leave her alive." Freddy lunged again but a thump to the back of his head sent him crashing to the floor. Mel cried out but the fat man held her close. "Idiots, did you think I would come without backup?" Another man stepped over Freddy and pointed his gun towards Joe. "Now, who's next?" The man actually laughed.

Two things happened next; Nick saw his chance and aimed at the man holding the gun to Joe, and without hesitation he took the shot. Mel, fearing for Joe's life, and wrapped in the fat man's arms, leant forward and then with all her might threw herself backwards, calling out, "You won't hurt my dad." The third gunman dropped his gun, clasping his shoulder where Nick's bullet had hit. Joe ran forwards and grabbed it off the floor. He didn't see what had happened behind him, didn't see what his daughter had done in a desperate act to save him, but Nick had a clear view of the whole thing. Mel had thrown herself backwards and the unsuspecting fat man had lost his balance and backed up to the wall that was now butting against his legs. The unbalanced weight had resulted in the two falling over the side.

Nick watched in horror as Mel's body fell, like in slow motion he saw every second of it, frame by frame, his whole body numb. Time stood still and he screamed silently as a tear escaped from his eye. As the tear fell down his cheek, Mel and the fat man fell from the bridge and as the tear left his cheek and hit the water with a silent splash, Mel hit the pebbled river beneath. The fat man having pushed himself away from Mel, they fell landed with a thud on the rocks to the bank; his body lay motionless and broken. Joe screamed as he leaned over the side of the bridge, realising what Mel had just done, his agonising cry echoing in the surrounding hills. Nick shook himself out of his shock-induced daze and after he regained feeling in his legs, rushed to get his beloved. The water fought him every step of the way, forcing him backwards but he pushed on through the current to get to her, wading knee deep in the shallows. He finally reached Mel dropping to his knees in the freezing cold water, her eyes were shut and her bright red hair was floating, gently swaying in the water around her head, indistinguishable from the blood red water that was flowing away from her and leaving trails like red ribbons as it rushed away downstream. "Mel" Nick called out, fighting the tears as he heard Joe's painful cries above him. "Mel, Mel, please open your eyes, please, Mel, don't leave me. I need you, I need to give you your forever." He shook her body in vain, Mel's eyes never opened.

Chapter 17

NICK SHIVERED AS he sat in the sparse waiting room that the hospital had ushered them all into, towels wrapped around his soaked legs. Rose and Alice sat either side of Nick, Rose clutching his hand in hers. Freddy and Joe sat opposite him in ripped old brown chairs staring at some imaginary speck on the green, shiny floor. Nell and Julian had brought Mr Michaels in earlier, but hearing about Mel they now joined everyone else to wait, Julian's arm was round Nell's waist and Nick could see she was leaning into him for support. He felt cold, emotionless; he could not allow himself to feel anything because once he did, the horror of what had happened would become real.

"Would you like a coffee or something, Nick?" Rose offered, Nick shook his head, fearing nothing would remain in his stomach. How had this happened? How cruel could fate be that he had finally fallen in love only to have her torn away from him?" His thoughts returned to Mel lying in the ice cold water, her luscious red hair flowing around her head framing her beautiful face, but her red hair had hidden the blood that poured out from her.

"Are you cold, son?" Joe asked, noticing him shivering. Again Nick shook his head, unable to speak. Freddy began tapping his foot, chewing on his fingernails.

"What the hell is taking so long?" he growled angrily. Joe patted his leg calming him. "I remember when we first brought her home," Freddy began "Do you remember, Joe? We didn't have a clue what to do with her," he laughed, and Joe smiled.

"I remember you suggesting we put her in the dog basket!" Joe sniffed.

"She probably would have loved that," Nick finally found his voice.

"She was so tiny; I thought I was going to break her every time I picked her up. She just used to look at me with those big puppy dog eyes as if to say that it was OK, she was OK. She couldn't even wrap her whole hand around my thumb. Do you remember?" Joe nodded as Freddy wrapped his hand around his thumb, demonstrating the move. The room fell silent again until Rose spoke.

"I remember you bringing her into the town hall," she said. "We couldn't believe it, a baby, but the minute I saw you both with her I knew she belonged to you. You were destined to be her family," she smiled sweetly as Freddy nodded; Joe swallowed hard, trying to stop the tears from swelling. "She's strong," Rose continued. "She will come back to us all, you will see." Nick lifted his head, there had been so much blood, so much all around her, flowing in the water round his legs where he knelt next to her. Could she recover? Would she ever be able to return to him? No one else spoke, there were no words that could console them all.

"Fred, Joe," the doctor acknowledged as he walked in, the two men stood and clasped hands with the doctor firmly. "Christ, it only seems two minutes ago I was bandaging Mel's arm when she fell out of that tree," he smiled warmly. "OK, she is still with us, that's good news, she is very strong." It seemed that everyone in the room let out a relieved sigh at the same time, clapping their hands together, but Nick remained still.

"But..." he started, the doctor nodded his head.

"Yes, the inevitable 'but'. Let me give you a breakdown of the damage. She has a broken wrist, broken ankle, I believe she may also have a number of broken ribs," he paused checking the chart in his hand. "There is a possibility of spinal injuries and in extreme cases brain damage but I stress that that is in extreme cases, the bridge she fell from was not high enough to cause those extreme types of injury, so I am hoping that none of this is applicable but it was a high fall, we won't know for sure until she regains consciousness."

"When might that be?" Joe asked timidly.

"Joe, I just don't know, she has had a massive trauma, she will be in a lot of pain when she does regain consciousness so it may be kinder to hope that she remains this way for a while until we can fully assess the injuries she has sustained." Joe nodded and thanked him. "Joe, I want to do a CT scan, we also need to check her spine. If there is any damage she may have to remain here for a while in a cast." He shuffled his feet uncomfortably "The problem is, all these tests, I can't do them with no paperwork, no history. I have to say I am out of my depth, lads; she will need to see specialists. I know we got away with it before but they were all little things, this...this is not something I can do on the sly or something I can do on my own. I'm sorry." Freddy ran his hand through his thinning light brown hair.

"Just fix her, whatever it takes," he pleaded.

"What if she was a private patient?" Nick interjected. "Would you need to take so many details?" The doctor looked at him then back at Freddy, who nodded his approval.

"We would have to take details, but I suppose I could make sure they weren't necessarily checked out. So long as the bills were paid." Again he looked to Freddy and Joe for confirmation.

"I will pay, put her down as a tourist; I will give you my details. I have enough money to cover everything that she needs, just do it." Nick stood to face the doctor eye to eye. "I will call my PA now and transfer funds." He reached into his pocket and pulled out his mobile and left to make the call, relieved that at last he could finally do something, it may be a small thing but it was better than just sitting around waiting. There was no debate with Mel, whatever she needed he would do. As he left, Nick didn't notice Joe cling to Freddy's arm as a single tear of stubborn gratitude fell from Freddy's eye.

"Freddy, there is also the matter of the police, they are sending someone over now, you need to decide what exactly you are going to tell them."

"Was anyone else admitted?" Joe asked. "A gunshot victim, arm wound?" The doctor shook his head. "OK, so no one saw what happened, in theory Mel could have been trying to save the fat man and his weight just carried them over the side." Freddy nodded at Joe in agreement. They could do this, if no one saw what had happened, who was to say that a crime was even committed? The doctor nodded to Freddy. "She has bruises on her arms that would confirm she was being held tightly, unfortunately, she also has strangulation marks." He was apologetic in his response. "Look I am sure it will all be OK, she has defensive wounds, they will prove that she was fighting for her life against someone, but the police will want to know why." He then turned his attention to Freddy. "Whether you like it or not, Fred, I need to check you out, that knock on your skull was quite bad and I need to see it." Freddy just growled at him, muttering something about doing it later. Sensing a fight brewing and seeing that Freddy was not dizzy or suffering blurry vision, he left them to their thoughts and carried on to see his other patients, making a note to pin him down before he left.

Melissa had been amazing, she transferred funds straight away, she then called the hospital advising them that they had a celebrity in the hospital. They were all to practice total discretion and not to discuss the incident with anyone. She threatened lawsuits for anyone who released information. No one asked them anymore questions after that. She had also called his mother who had immediately got into her car and set off to support her son. By the time he returned to the waiting room everything had been sorted out, and he was back to sitting in that dull room and just waiting.

"Listen, there is no point in everyone waiting here," he told them. "You should go home and we will call you as soon as we hear news." No one left, though.

"Nick, she is our family too," Rose began.

"I realise that I didn't mean..." he began, but Rose silenced him by raising her hand.

"I know exactly what you meant, boy, but let me say to you, you are not an island. Mel loves you and that makes you family. We are not just here for Mel!" Hearing her words spoken so soundly finally broke him. Nick collapsed on the floor, sobbing his heart out. Nell and Rose rushed to hold him, the two women enveloping him in a cocoon, protecting him. He couldn't stop, tears fell like fountains crashing onto the cold hard floor where he sat. He couldn't lose her, wouldn't lose her. His world would collapse without Mel; she had protected them right up until the last minute, protecting Joe from the men that captured her. Nick scrubbed his eyes clear long

enough to look over at Joe, he knew
how guilty he felt, he knew that Joe would have given his life for his precious daughter but it was not his fault. The man at fault was dead and Nick was glad, he could never hurt Mel ever again. The sight of his twisted body pleased Nick, and though Nick had never had a malicious thought in his life before, he hoped the fat man had died in pain for the damage he had done and for the pain he had caused his beautiful woman.

A tall, thin nurse opened the door to the waiting room. "You can go see her now if you like," she announced. "Only two visitors," she added harshly as Freddy, Joe and Nick all stood up together.

"You go," Freddy said to Joe and Nick, slowly sitting down again.

"No, she would want you," Nick replied. "You two were her world, you still are her world. I ...well, I've just known her a short time." His face fell as he spoke, but Freddy snorted.

"Don't kid yourself," he said sternly. "I know my girl loves you, I may not like it, but I know it!" His gruff voice and the way he spoke begrudgingly made Nick smile. She loved him, he knew it and now it would seem Freddy knew it too. The three stood in the middle of the room in silent acknowledgement, but it was Alice that spoke first.

"Mary Louise Tyler, I have known you since you came into the café in pigtails! Now don't be so ridiculous, it makes absolutely no difference whatsoever whether there are two people or three in that room. So just step aside and let these men in to see her!" With her speech donc Alice sat back down, folding her arms into her lap. Rose looked at her sideways as if she didn't know who she was. The girl stood stunned in the doorway. "Don't you dare make me tell your father about the time I caught you in my veg patch with that lad from the next village!" she continued. The nurse opened her mouth, aghast at the audacity of the old woman, then realising that she was being serious and would in fact tell her father exactly what she was doing with Timmy Jake that day, nodded and invited all three to follow her. Julian grinned from his position seated across the room.

"I knew all that acid was stored up in you for some reason" he chuckled, she just sneered at him but didn't dignify him with a response. Instead she opted to dig around in her handbag and pull out a bag of sweets that she didn't offer to anyone else, just helped herself to one then wrapped them back up, placing her bag back on the floor, a smug expression plastered to her wrinkled, weathered face.

Mel lay in a crisp white bed, her shocking, red hair was tucked away behind her, machines beeped and tubes and wires tied her to them. Joe clasped his hands over his mouth when he saw her; Freddy remained stationary in the doorway, unable to enter, needing the frame for support. Nick walked

around to the other side of the bed
and sat down on a small orange chair placed there
by the nurse.

"Hey, baby," he whispered tenderly. "How you
doing? Everyone is here for you, they are all outside
waiting to hear how you are, so don't you keep them
waiting long!" Joe pulled the chair out at the other
side but Freddy remained standing like a stone
statue. Nick continued. "Nell is going to check in on
Millie and the puppies, so don't worry, and Mr
Michaels is being kept in overnight then he can go
home, so there is nothing for you to worry about."

"Yes, that's right," Joe confirmed. "Even Freddy's
here and you know how much he hates hospitals!"
He took up her hand and tried to find some skin that
he could stroke without a tube coming out of it. His
breathing shuddered as he stroked her fingers,
fighting the urge to cry again. Nick took over. "Even
Alice is here, she's causing trouble with the nursing
staff but she's here!" he laughed, "My mum is on her
way too, she wants so much to meet you, Mel, so you
have to open your eyes. You have to fight, baby,
cause I can't ..." He couldn't speak any more, his
heart was in a million pieces, his life would be
worthless if she wasn't in it. Joe reached over the
bed and held Nick's hand. "She looks like she is just
sleeping," Nick whispered, his voice cracked as tears
unashamedly fell.

"I knew you had fallen in love the minute I saw
you!" Joe told Nick. "You just had to look at Mel and
your eyes were alight and sparkly and she was just

the same. She's never really had a man in her life, not for long, anyway. I think that was our fault." He released Nick's hand and began chewing the corner of his thumb nail. "You see, we were always so protective of her, only allowed a few people to know anything about her. We stopped her having a life." Nick began to disagree. "No it's true, but then you arrived, Nick, and she just seemed to click, she wanted to tell you all about herself, all her defences dropped. She must really love you, more than we thought." He turned to look at Freddy.

"I don't need to listen to this crap," he growled, and stormed away from the room.

"He doesn't like hospitals," Joe defended. "Mel was always in them you see, she fell over, crashed things, got bitten, it was never-ending. I just accepted it, I mean she was a kid, that's what they do, but Freddy, he blamed everything on himself, everything was because he had failed somehow." Joe stroked Mel's cheek as he spoke, tenderly brushing from one side to the other. Nick listened silently, what could he say? Mel knew her dads loved her; she had talked to him about them, how wonderful they were. Nick had always been intimidated by them, well by Freddy, but now he understood. They were her guardians, her protectors and they would do whatever they needed to do to keep her safe, not just safe but happy.

"I love her so much," Nick blurted out again, "I can't explain it, I just know that I want to be with her. She is a remarkable woman, Joe; you raised a truly amazing woman. I don't know what I will do if she..." Joe silenced him.

"Don't say that!" he yelled. "Don't ever say that. Mel needs us to be strong, be here as a family for her. She is going to wake up and she is going to be fine!" Joe broke down uttering the last words, and Freddy came running from around the corner where he had been skulking. Not hesitating, he rushed to Joe's side, kneeling next to him their two heads touched together and they sat both looking towards Mel. It was the first time Nick had seen them be affectionate towards each other, they were usually fighting or taking the 'mickey' out of him whenever he had seen them. This was different; Freddy held Joe's hand and the two men sat as Joe wept. It made Nick's heart yearn watching them, he needed Mel to be OK, she had to be, he stood up to leave the two men to their private moment.

"Where the hell do you think you're going?" Freddy bawled.

"I was just going to give you a moment," he muttered.

"Are we making you uncomfortable?"

"Freddy, stop it!" Joe demanded as Freddy rose to his feet. "This is not what Mel needs."

"You are making me uncomfortable," Nick admitted defiantly. "But not because of the reasons you think. Because you have what I want, I want to have Mel in my arms, I want to comfort her with just a look or a single touch like you and Joe do with each other. I want..." angry tears pushed their way forward annoying Nick more. "I want to have Mel alive and well. I want to take her on picnics and visit Heavens Point like she wanted to. I want to have her show me all the wonderful secret places she knows in the village. I want her to sit and sketch in that old book of hers. I want to argue and fight and make up... and I can't...I don't know if I will ever get to do any of these things. I am angry because you had so much time with her and I had so little. I am angry because I wanted to save her...and I couldn't...I just couldn't." He stormed past Freddy but Freddy caught him by the elbow.

"Stay," he mumbled quietly, "please," he added, releasing Nick by the elbow, not able to look at him. "She needs all of us."

Chapter 18

NICK'S MOTHER ARRIVED less than two hours after he had called Melissa, turning up looking immaculate as always, she had demanded to know where her son was. She was directed to the dull, dreary room and had waited with the others until Nick finally came out of Mel's room looking tired and exhausted. Diane wasted no time in hugging her son, who barely managed to hug her back. A police officer stood waiting for him and the two fathers as they left the room.

He asked who it was that had been hurt; Freddy had explained that she was his daughter from a previous relationship and that she had lived with them both from an early age. The police officer then asked them about the victim.

"I have no idea who he was," Freddy lied.

"No, I have never seen him either." Joe confirmed. The officer looked between the two.

"So what was it exactly that made you go up to the bridge in the first place?"

Nick spoke up. "They were giving me a lift." His voice was quiet and timid but he tried to clear it. "I had arranged to meet her there, it was a surprise." he swallowed hard and stared at his feet.

"And you are?"

"This is Nick Mill-Thorpe." Joe spoke out for him. "He is my daughter's boyfriend." The officer continued to ask questions but all the villagers were sticking to the same story, no one knew the man, no one had ever seen him before and Mel had simply been going to the bridge to meet her boyfriend. The doctor had shown the officer the bruises and wounds on the girl's face and hands, and so he could only presume that the fat man had got rough with her and they had toppled over the side. There was no other evidence to suggest the contrary. He could pursue it further but why bother; if all parties were happy he could write this up and get home in time for tea.

"What an absolute load of horse poo!" Nick's mother said, as soon as she was sure the officer had left. "You had better tell me the truth, young man." Nick looked over to Joe, who nodded. Diane sat and patiently listened as Nick tried to explain exactly what had happened to his beloved Mel. Tried to explain who she was and how she had ended up in hospital. His mother sat quietly and listened intently, trying to digest all the information Nick was throwing at her. Nick feared her reaction, feared that she would demand that he return with her immediately and leave Mel, but he could not leave her, and would not be forced to choose between his mother and his love.

"So you have all hidden her, all this time?" Diane addressed everyone in the waiting room, they all nodded nervously. Her eyes fixed onto Nell, "I know you, don't I?" Nell nodded.

"We ran a few restaurants and bars that George used to frequent, a while ago now of course," she mumbled, trying to clear her throat. Diane nodded in acknowledgement; she then turned to her son who anxiously waited for her verdict.

"It's quite a story isn't it?" She spoke quietly to him, then after a long painful pause added, "This must be a wonderful village and community for everyone to agree to protect this girl, you have kept her safe her whole life." She looked around the room, amazed at how this community had all come together to protect a stranger, that would never happen in the city. "She must be a very special young woman," she added kindly. Nick's eyes could cry no more but the pain he felt hearing his mother's words surged through every nerve.

"I..." Nick began but couldn't speak, couldn't find his voice to say all the things he wanted to say, couldn't find the voice to tell his mother just what a wonderful person Mel was, and that if she did know she would never question the villagers' decision to protect her, he would lay his life down for Mel. His face contorted with the emotion he failed to express.

"It's OK, son, it's OK," she soothed. "So, can I meet her?" Nick nodded slowly.

Diane held her composure well as she walked into the grief-filled room where Mel lay. Not that she didn't feel horrified by everything, but because she needed to give her son the strength that he could not muster for himself.

"Mum, this is Freddy and Joe, Mel's fathers." Freddy stood to shake Diane's hand and Joe forced a smile. Diane retrieved her hand and rubbed it slightly where Freddy had squeezed a little too hard unconsciously, *obviously not a man used to shaking the hand of a woman*, she thought.

"So you are the one who dumped us with their son!" Freddy attempted to lighten the situation.

"So you are the one who's been giving my son grief for simply falling in love!" she retaliated with a dry smile. Joe snorted in delight at Freddy getting his long overdue 'comeuppance'. Diane moved around to the side of the bed and gently began stroking Mel's hair. "She will need her wash things, and her makeup," she began. "Nick, a woman needs her little comforts, when she wakes up she will want to make herself feel better, we women self-heal." Nick nodded.

"She has everything in her bag;" but when he glanced around he realised her bag must still be in the shop where she started her day off. "Oh God, no, she hasn't, her bag, her bag is not here. It must be at Mr Michaels', but it will be locked up, I can't get to it and she needs it but..." It seemed a silly thing to panic over but he knew that Mel took her bag everywhere; she had her life in that bag.

"I will go get it," Freddy offered. "I'm no good sitting around here anyway." Joe agreed.

"Would you get her book, please?" Nick asked. "Her sketch book under her bed, I would like to show my mum and I think she will need it when she wakes up." Freddy nodded and left the room, kissing Mel on the forehead before he left. "She has this book," Nick explained to his mother. "It has sketches of everyone she loves in it."

"And are you in it?" his mother asked. Nick smiled timidly and Diane returned it happily.

"It's not just that, she has this tree in it." At hearing this, Joe let out a little laugh.

"Oh my God, I had forgotten about that bloody tree," he smiled fondly. "She was such a wild child, Diane, I cannot begin to tell you, temper like you wouldn't believe."

"Oh you don't need to tell me," Diane chimed in, "this one used to hold his breath until he was purple just to get his own way!" Joe laughed and Nick rolled his eyes.

"We came up with this idea, you see, she would sketch this tree, bare with no leaves. I would then set the book up in front of her and she would stare at it, I would tell her to imagine blossom growing on each branch, each one slowly opening and blooming. She would sit there for hours, her little face all screwed up as she concentrated until she could see the whole tree in full bloom and by then...well she was all calm again."

"That's a fantastic idea," Diane crooned. "I timed Nick out all the time, grounded him, nothing ever worked. Then he became a teenager and never spoke to us for about three years unless it was a grunt or groan." Joe now spoke enthusiastically.

"I know, I know...I swear they have their own language," he chuckled. Nick decided to stay out of this conversation but somehow the fact that his mum and Joe were chatting away happily gave him a strange little warm feeling, a feeling that radiated through his chest.

"She is very lucky having two wonderful parents in her life," Diane commended Joe. "It was so hard when Nick's father died, on all of us." She removed a handkerchief from her sleeve to dab her weeping eyes. Nick took her hand but could offer no comfort.

"She tried to save me." It was Joe now who was crying. "I thought by my actions that I was saving her, but in that split second she had saved me instead." He sobbed now, his chest heaving. "I am the parent, it was my job not hers, I should have ..." Joe broke down and Diane rushed to his side to comfort him.

"She's not a kid anymore; she loves you so much, I can tell that just by listening to you talk about her. She tried to save everyone, she protected her family,

you can never be sad about that,
Joe, you should be proud." Diane's words did not
settle Joe, who just stared at his daughter as she lay
lifeless in the stark white bed.

Freddy returned promptly with a large bag filled
with all Mel's things; well, everything he could find
spread across numerous addresses anyway,
everything that she needed and a whole load of
things she would probably never need. He had told
everyone that was left to go home, and promised
that he would call with any news and eventually the
waiting room emptied. Joe entered the room with a
hot cup of coffee and handed it over to him. "You
need that bump looking at Fred," Joe scolded.

"I don't think I can do this anymore, Joe," he
confessed, not able to look him in the eye. "This is
our baby and I cannot do anything! I can't do
ANYTHING!" His anger and rage bubbled to the
surface and he threw the cup with all his might
across the room. The coffee sprayed over the wall in
a brown splatter mark then slowly trickled down
the walls, leaving long brown streaks. Joe sighed
heavily, he had seen Freddy like this before and it
was not a foregone conclusion as to whether he
would calm down or not. Silently he bent down and
began collecting the shattered pieces of cup from the
floor and under the chairs, working conscientiously,
listening to the rapid, heavy breaths that Freddy
was taking. As he collected the final tiny piece he
sliced it through his finger accidently.

"Shit" he called out, sitting back on his heels, shaking the pain from his finger. Freddy appeared at his side instantly, kneeling next to him.

"Let me see," he instructed.

"It s nothing, just leave it," Joe retorted but Freddy looked at him, sorrow and sadness radiating from his big brown eyes. Joe surrendered his hand over and Freddy checked to make sure no shards were imbedded.

"I'm sorry," he whispered, stroking Joe's hand gently.

Freddy always ran when they needed him, leaving Joe to deal with all life's traumas. When they had become more than friends when they were kids, Freddy had wanted to run, leave everyone behind before anyone found out, but Joe had made him stay and face their parents together. It was true that both their families had been furious with them and tried to split them up, send them away, but Joe had stayed resident and eventually Freddy had stood next to him, shoulder to shoulder they had fought their families and though they had eventually left, they had left on their own terms, not the families'. Joe had been so happy with Freddy that day, he had defended him and if possible it had brought them even closer together, but Freddy still had that flight instinct and it worried Joe sometimes. But now they had Mel to think of and he would not allow Freddy to run from their daughter.

"Fred, she needs you! You can't keep running away when things get tough." Joe spoke strongly.

"I know. I am gonna try, Joe." He turned Joe's face so that they were looking directly into each other's eyes. "I am, I promise. I am gonna be here more for you, for you both." Joe smiled.

"Liar" he chuckled. A small cough startled them both, causing Freddy to leap up and stand at the other side of the room.

"I am sorry, I don't mean to intrude." Diane began grinning as she spoke. Freddy frowned at her as she laughed. "You remind me so much of Nick's father, when we first started going out, he would not even stand near me if we were out." She turned to Joe. "The first time I kissed him in public he practically broke out in a sweat." Joe returned her grin, acknowledging that Freddy was just the same. Diane turned to Freddy. "You shouldn't worry, though, if Joe is anything like me he knows how much you care deep down." Freddy stared at Diane, deciding whether she was mocking him or not, but she just continued to smile, a sadness shadowing her smile. "You see, you offer the strength that Joe needs and Joe, he gives you the words that you are unable to find. Two halves of the same whole, that's what my husband used to say." She looked between the two who were now both clearing the wedged emotion from their throats. "What am I thinking? Sorry, Nick wanted me to ask you if you brought Mel's books in. He wants to show me Mel's drawings of everyone, if that's OK? I realise it is personal so if it's not OK I understand." Freddy nodded and handed over the bag. "He seems to be a little nervous of you," she questioned in Freddy's direction. "I cannot think why?" she called over her shoulder as she left. Joe let out a giggle and Freddy shot him a look.

"You better get used to him, Freddy, you know as well as I do that boy has her heart now." Freddy just grunted.

Diane thought the pictures were amazing, each person had been drawn in such detail, every line had been drawn with such care, it was pure love in those drawings. Nick felt a strong sense of pride as his mother gushed over every picture that she perused in that battered old book of Mel's. She paused as she reached the sketch Mel had done of Nick and gasped slightly, she stroked the page affectionately. "You look so much like you father," she sniffed, "it's as if she knew him, she has captured him in you, look, look at the eyes, they are the very image of your father's." Her fingers glided over the picture.

"She was always good at her drawings," Freddy explained as he and Joe entered the room again. "She would be in the fields with me all day long, I would see this field that needed ploughing or a tractor that needed repairing, but Mel..." he took a breath, looking over to the bed "...she would see so much more. Every flower, every creature and beast. She even got me to take this bloody great big ginger cow cause someone didn't want it. Have you seen it?" Nick laughed, explaining to his mother who Fred the highland cow was. "Even named it after me!"

"Can't think what she thought the similarities were," Joe chipped in.

"They are both beautiful," a tiny voice spoke out. Everyone turned to the bed as Mel desperately tried to open her eyes. She could hear them all talking and wanted to join in, wanted to come back to them but her eyelids were just so heavy. She was so tired and the pain, the pain was unbearable, she just wanted to go back to her peaceful sleep. Nick held his breath, not daring to move, Joe and Diane both had their hands over their mouths, but still Mel could not open her eyes. Freddy stepped up to the bed.

"You need to come back now, girl," he spoke in a determined voice. "We need you, we can't see the blossoms on that bloody tree of yours, you need to be here to make it bloom." Nick stared mesmerised as this huge man spoke to his tiny fragile daughter.

"Maybe we should let her rest," Diane suggested but Freddy leant in and whispered something into Mel's ear. He sat back and waited. Slowly so slowly, Mel's eyelashes began to flutter and after what seemed like an eternity they opened just the tiniest little bit, but as she did the room blossomed.

It took several minutes for Mel to fully wake up, the doctors and nurses fussed around her checking all the machines and shining lights in her already sore eyes. Through all the kerfuffle Nick just sat in the chair, a contented smile etched into his face. His heart had begun to beat again.

Diane and Joe went to get more coffee but Freddy refused to leave his daughter's side. Diane and Joe had shared a knowledgeable smile that Freddy was excluded from, and left chatting away about where Diane was going to stay whilst she was in the village.

"I'm tired," Mel managed to mutter as Freddy held the cup of water to her lips, allowing her a small sip.

"Of course you are, girl!" he chastised. "You just fell off a bloody great big bridge and if you ever put me through that again I am getting rid of Fred! FOR GOOD!" he threatened. Mel just blinked heavily, knowing he would never get rid of Fred, she had seen him talking to him on the cold nights he was out checking all the other beasts, talking to him like he was an old friend. She turned to Nick, who was fixed onto her other side, her hand wrapped tightly in his.

"I'm sorry," she murmured.

"What on earth are you sorry for?" he asked confused.

"I am going to cause you so much stress, just look what I do to him!" She nodded over to Freddy and the two men laughed.

"I think I can handle it," he assured her.

"Forever?"

A tear fell from Nick's eyes and he kissed the top of her hand. "Forever and then some." Mel smiled, and allowed her eyes to close. Nick brushed her fringe away from her eyes and listened to the gentle sound of her sleepy breathing.

"I keep telling her to get it cut," Freddy muttered, watching the intimate gesture awkwardly. The way Nick had brushed her hair away from her eyes was the exact same thing that Joe used to do to him. They would work long hours out in the fields, desperately trying to earn enough money to set up on their own. Joe would pull out a flask of tea and the two would sit next to each other on the side of the tractor or hay bale. Freddy would always apologise for putting him through this and tell Joe to just go home where he wouldn't have to work so hard, but Joe would always lean over and brush his hair away, telling him that he was worth it. It would always make Freddy's heart tingle and he would feel so proud, and now he was sitting here watching Nick do the same for his little girl. Maybe he would have to get used to this boy after all.

The nurse entered the room and, quite rudely, advised them to leave whilst Mel got some rest. Both men agreed then, instead of taking the nurse's suggestion and heading home, both headed towards the waiting room, occupying seats at opposite ends of the deserted space.

"Fred, can I ask you something?" Nick began.

"If it is for my daughter's hand in marriage, you can forget it," Freddy bellowed, Nick held back a smug smile, realising that he was getting to the man but he needed to know.

"What did you say to her? You whispered something to Mel and you brought her back, what did you say to her that made her open her eyes?" Freddy snarled, and his teeth appeared in a sinister grin.

"I told her that if she didn't wake up then she could no longer protect you from me. If she wasn't around then I would blame you and that would make you fair game!"

"That's what brought her back?" Nick was astounded. Freddy's grin faltered.

"That's what made her fight," he corrected. "I guess she thinks you are worth it."

Chapter 19

"MR MILL-THORPE, I loved your book." Nick sat behind a large desk, signing copies of his new book. His audience had changed somewhat with his second book and the line of fans now consisted of a wider range of people. He still had his young fans, but he also had a new fan base of people who loved his writing now, not just his looks.

"So, Mr Mill-Thorpe, what do think to the rumours of your latest book being made into a movie?" Nick looked at the young man standing opposite.

"I would love to see that happen," he smiled genuinely "...but I'm afraid no one has talked to me yet." The young man beamed.

"Only a matter of time."

Melissa had a full buffet laid out for Nick as he finished up in the book store, plates of pies, sandwiches and burgers stood next to colourful plates of salads and fruit selections. Nick smiled at the array of colours before him.

"Did I do good or did I do good?" Melissa called out behind him.

"Yeah, Melissa, you did good. Don't you think it looks pretty?" he asked. "All the colours and that." Melissa frowned at him.

"Pretty? What an earth happened to you? You got weird," she mocked, shoving a small meat pie into her mouth. "What happened to the boy who just wanted to sit around in his pants and eat burgers and watch TV?" Nick wrapped his arm around her waist and kissed her on the top of her head.

"He grew up and realised what a lazy, selfish git he had been and how wonderful his agent was to him." Melissa looked up at him and chuckled, pulling him into a tight cuddle, she really did love this man, he was above all else her favourite client and friend. She was so proud of him and the fact that he was now becoming the man that she had seen that he could be as he sat, a gangly teenager with scruffy notebooks, all those years ago.

Nick had not gone on to write a sequel to his first book as promised, much to the disappointment of his fans, not to mention his publisher, but he had assured them of a new book and he had delivered. The spy novel, 'Caramel', was proving to have all the qualities of a best seller and had received fantastic reviews so far. The sexy story of a girl with no identity caught up in the criminal world had captured the imagination of thousands.

"So what time are you leaving?" Melissa asked, filling her plate with delicious morsels. Since Nick's return, he had grown up and taken on all the duties

associated with fame with a new
found vigour. She no longer had to fight with him
over interviews or appearances. Nick went gladly,
and with his new audience he could talk about his
work passionately and was offered interviews with
genuine book lovers. Life was a lot easier now, that
was for sure, so long as Nick could return home
regularly he would do whatever was required, he
had managed to find that dividing line that gave him
a life outside the public eye.

"When I have demolished this amazing food,"
Nick responded to her question. "Is it me or have the
perks of book signings got better with this new
book? I mean we used to get a few stale sandwiches,
now we get this fantastic spread." His plate now
began to overflow with food. Everything looked so
delicious, he wanted to try everything all at once.

"Yes and no," Melissa offered. "Yes, perks have
got better, you are being seen as a professional
writer now, not just a one hit wonder, but no, this
wasn't arranged by the book store." She smiled.
"Cam organised all this, I tell you, no one dare say a
bad word against you when she is around, she
worships the ground you walk on!" She rolled her
eyes. Nick remembered how upset Cam had been
when she had been attacked by her supposed
boyfriend. He had stayed with her until she was safe
at home; he asked Melissa to thank her and send
some flowers from him to show his appreciation.

"Yes, boss," she teased. "Anyway, she has a new
love now; she met this guy on the internet and

believes he may be the one. The fact that he likes your books probably has something to do with it."

"That's great but is that safe, over the internet?" He worried about her, women just weren't safe these days.

"That is how it is done these days, just cause you went on a road trip and found love!" She giggled at the soppy look on his face. "Incidentally, I too have a man in my life, if you are interested." Nick spat crumbs onto his plate.

"What?" he muttered with a mouthful of food still. "When? Who? Why didn't you tell me?"

Melissa blushed. "Well it's this guy from a big publishers, he asked me out and well, it's going well. Your Uncle George is insisting that we all go out for dinner tonight so he can get to know him." Nick chuckled, if she was letting George meet him he must be the one, George would tear him apart in seconds if he wasn't genuine.

It was nice spending a bit of time with Melissa, since the accident he had spent as much time as possible in the Dales, refusing to leave Mel until she was well. The police had not really pursued the matter; as soon as the body was identified the local officer had been inundated with praise. Commendations were offered and the story very quickly turned into a fable about a local officer who had seen a suspicious character and acted upon it, following him only to arrive too late. He had accepted all the praise that was offered to him and so next to the story of a big criminal's death, Mel's identity was never questioned.

Nick had taken his laptop into the hospital every day, discussing what he was writing and telling her all about the plots. Mel had insisted that his main female character be tough and strong and be able to take care of herself. He had no need to be persuaded; he simply had to look at the amazing strong woman fighting pain every day sitting right in front of him. They had spent hours researching martial arts, deciding what skills she should have, and reading autobiographies and real life stories to decide how she would act and behave, Mel really did have a vivid imagination and produced remarkable and exciting ideas. Nick had never been so happy in his life and with all his professional commitments taken care of, now he needed to get home to her.

As soon as Nick's car pulled up outside Pine Tree Cottage, frantic barking could be heard from within, the pups that had been temporary guests at first had now somehow become permanent residents. They were loud but no one seemed to mind, especially the farmer next door, he had had the audacity to complain about the noise once but Mel had interjected and told him that they were loud to scare off the foxes. This response seemed to please him, and he had actually shook Nick's hand and never bothered him again.

"Alright, alright let me get in the door!" he objected, throwing his bags onto the sofa. He immediately picked up the little black pup whose life he had held in his hands when it had been born. Nick had thought the pup would never breathe, but when it had finally let out that first hiccup it had buried its way into his heart. The pup nuzzled his neck and licked his face frantically; his lips were pulled back into that telltale smile that it only did when Nick came home. Freddy thought he was pathetic and told him so, but Nick didn't care, this little pup was his baby. "How's my boy? How's my boy?" he gushed as the little pup squirmed in his arms, the other two pups danced around his feet, not willing to wait for their turn. Eventually the pups returned to their beds, satisfied that their dad was home to stay, and Nick walked into the kitchen area to make a cup of tea. He wondered where Mel was today. He had long since given up trying to locate her, she popped in and out when he was away to see to the pups but trying to find her when he wanted to was a nightmare, better to let her find him.

As he sat in the garden with his pot of tea and his feet up, the pups began barking again, a high pitched excited bark that could only mean one thing. "Oh for heaven's sake, get down, get down now. You really are the naughtiest pups I have ever known, do you know that!" Nick stood in the doorway, watching her trying to enter the house whilst the pups jumped all over her. She walked slowly and her leg was still a little crooked, giving her a slight limp. Nick knew she still found it painful but would never say so. She turned to see Nick and dived into his arms.

"When did you get back?" she asked, not allowing him to respond because she immediately kissed him. He melted against her as he always did, holding his cup out to the side away from her. He missed her so much when he was away but he knew she needed time away from him. When he stayed in the village she rarely left the house, choosing to stay with him every night and that was a real blessing to him, an honour of sorts. He also understood that it was strange for her to remain in one place for so long, so the trips that he took allowed her to have space to be herself and be where she wanted to be. Not that he would mind her staying away when he was home, but she was content to stay. Nick was so frightened of scaring her, of her feeling trapped, so he would purposely organise trips he didn't necessarily have to do, to ensure Mel was happy.

Nick's hobby had turned into watching Mel like a hawk, watching for any change in behaviour or facial expression that might indicate that she had itchy feet and needed a bit of space. The minute he saw any signs he would invent a trip that took him away for a few days, she would kill him if she ever found out, but he didn't care, he loved this woman heart and soul, and the pain he felt every time he left her paled into comparison to the welcome he received when he came home.

"I missed you so much," she whispered into his mouth.

"Me too."

"Fancy a long hot bath?" she asked, Nick laughed.

"You only want me for my bath!" he pouted, Mel pulled him close.

"I can have your bath anytime I want, I do have a key." She wiggled her keys in front of him "What I can't have at any time is you in it," and taking his hand she led him up the stairs the same way she had nearly a year ago. Of course this time three puppies scampered up after them, jostling with each other to get into the lead.

Joe greeted Nick warmly as he got out of the car with Mel; Freddy stood in the doorway and nodded gloomily. "Since when do we entertain?" he had complained when Joe had told them that Mel and Nick were coming over for dinner. He had nearly had a heart attack when he added under his breath that Diane and Mr Michaels were also coming.

"Dad!" Mel called out and hugged Freddy.

"How's the ankle?" Freddy asked, watching her favour her other foot as she stood.

"It's good, Dad, physio is going well and I will be running around before you know it." She kissed him on the cheek and he just grunted.

"Ignore him, he's grouchy," Joe explained, although no explanation was required when it came to Freddy. He leant in to whisper to Nick, "So your mum and Mr Michaels are already here." Nick looked at him, confused; his mother had not mentioned anything about coming up. Joe continued, "It would appear that whilst we were all sitting by Mel's bedside that night, your mother was visiting Mr Michaels, keeping him company; it would appear that your mother has been visiting Mr Michaels quite a lot over the last few months." This was all news to him; his mother had not mentioned anything about him to Nick. Joe grinned, he was becoming such a gossipmonger.

Freddy stood and carved the beef joint up at the head of the table, it was not as if he would have let anyone else do it! Nick's mother had embraced him warmly, if a little shyly. Mr Michaels had actually smiled at him! Mel looked happy; she sat eating the amazing fresh food and chatted to everyone excitedly about Nick's success. He didn't say a word, he just listened to Mel tell everyone about how well he had done and how brilliant his story was, so intricate and how it kept you guessing right up until the very end. Freddy had remained silent but Mr Michaels had actually been interested, asking him about parts of the story.

"Oh my God, have you actually read it?" Nick asked, surprised.

"Of course I have, well, your mother has been reading parts of it to me as I work in the shop and..." He stopped abruptly, fearing he had said something wrong. Diane began intensely cutting up her meat, avoiding Nick's glance.

"So where have you been staying, Mother? I mean, you don't stay at Uncle George's cottage so where is it you stay all these times you have been visiting?" The table was silent, everyone looking at each other warily. It was Freddy that finally broke the awkwardness.

"Ha! Now you know how I feel!" he hooted. Mel grinned and looked into her plate. Diane's face was now scarlet. Nick managed to smile, he was happy for his mother, she deserved to be happy, but Mr Michaels - seriously?

"I have no intention of making Mr Michaels feel the way you make me feel, Freddy!" he spat out. "I am glad you are happy, Mum." Diane smiled and Mr Michaels held her hand over the table.

"I am," she said gingerly. Freddy pretended to put his fingers down his throat and gag at all the sentimentality. They all returned to their meal and Mel returned to her chatter, changing the subject now to farming matters, a subject she knew Freddy would not shut up about.

Epilogue

THE SUN SHONE brightly as Nick looked out over the Dales, his hair blew in the cool breeze that danced around him, cooling him from the ferocious heat. Mel had always wanted to take him to Heavens Point, wanted to show him how beautiful it was, she had understated its beauty. The view that Nick took in was nothing short of Heaven itself, the colourful hills rolled on in every direction, a slight mist covering the ground like fluffy clouds that had fallen from the skies and rested, hovering weightlessly.

"Nick," his mother called out to him. She arrived on the arm of Mr Michaels; the two a permanent couple now, Nick was overjoyed to see his mother so happy. Diane was often to be found behind the counter in Mr Michaels' shop, organising cans of produce or arranging delicate displays. They shared so much in common and whilst he would never replace his father, Diane had found love again.

"You ready, boy?" Uncle George called out. Nick's stomach twisted into knots, he couldn't do this, it wasn't right. Diane noticed the colour draining from his face and the slight sway he displayed, and stood to his side to steady him.

"I love you, Nick," she whispered. "I am so proud of you, I know you are nervous now, sweetheart, but that is soon going to all disappear, trust me." She pulled at his tie to lower him to a position where she could reach his forehead, and kissed him. "It's going to be OK."

His mother was right, for at that moment he saw his angel walking towards him, Joe on one side and Freddy on the other. Mel was a vision in purple silk that billowed around her in the breeze; she looked like she was floating. And just like that, all Nick's worries disappeared, his nerves vanished and all that mattered was the smile that his beautiful Mel had on her face.

"Are you insane?" Freddy and Joe had shouted when Nick had first talked to them about his idea. "She has no legal status, she doesn't even have a birth certificate, how the hell can you even think about this?" the two men had thundered for several minutes. Nick was relieved that Mel was in the village today as he was sure the men's voices could be heard all the way across the farm.

"Listen for two minutes please," he attempted but Freddy was having none of it. "Tell me you haven't mentioned it to Mel, do you know how this is going to break her heart, you little...." Joe did not let him finish.

"Let him talk," Joe said, suddenly calming down as he saw the seriousness in Nick's eyes.

Nick cleared his throat ready to recite the speech he had practiced a hundred times already. "I don't just want a wedding, I want a marriage. A wedding

is not just about the paperwork and
the day, I want more than that for Mel and I want it
without all the paperwork!" That's when he knew he
had Joe on board. Joe bit his thumbnail nervously as
he listened, then looked over at Freddy hopefully.
Spurred on, Nick continued, "...a wedding is words of
love spoken in front of people that you love and who
love you. It doesn't have to have a legality to it, it
just has to be a day of celebration, a celebration of
two people loving each other." He paused, allowing
Freddy to digest the information, "I do love her,
Freddy, so much. I want her to have the forever she
has dreamed of." That was it, Joe had gone, tears
poured down his face and his hand was clutched
over his heart. Freddy looked at the joy in the eyes
of the man he loved, he did not stand a chance of
opposing this.

"I am not her keeper, it's up to Mel whether she
wants you or not," and that was the best Nick was
going to get from Freddy. Joe leapt up excitedly and
began planning, immediately calling Diane to
arrange a meeting.

"You look beautiful," Nick managed, a lump
forming in his throat. Mel smiled shyly.

Joe kissed her on the cheek and handed her over
to Nick, she turned to Freddy who bit his lip,
unwilling to let go.

"Look, this is far from a conventional wedding, so
why don't you just stay up here with us," Nick

offered, realising that Freddy was not moving. Mel was having none of it.

"You have to let me go now, Dad," Mel told him gently. "It's time to let me go." Freddy kissed her hand. "You will always be my princess," he mumbled, adding "and if he ever hurts you I will knock his lights out." Joe grabbed him, embarrassed, and dragged him to sit down, scolding him quietly as he did. Freddy did not care, he had said his piece and that was that.

Everyone in the village had helped with the wedding plans; it had been Mr Michaels who had suggested having the ceremony at Heavens Point. He knew it was Mel's favourite place and she had been upset that she couldn't hike up to it whenever she wanted to anymore. Her ankle hindered her and she needed help at various points of the climb. Mr Michaels had thought that if she had wedding photos of it then she would not miss it so much. Nick had hugged him at this wonderful suggestion and thanked him for looking after her and his mum. Mr Michaels had smiled uncomfortably and quickly disappeared into the shop to organise cans. White chairs were lined up, creating an aisle for Mel to walk down, and buttercups had been gathered into any possible vessel and scattered around. Mel was right; the buttercups really did light up the sky, creating a warm yellow glow all around them. Of course Uncle George's friend, Billy, had insisted that as he played a vicar in a long running play he was the most qualified to conduct the mock ceremony and had arrived in a full vicar costume. Uncle George was very dapper in a dark suit; of course it did not hide the vibrant bright orange socks that poked out from the bottom.

Everyone sat down as Billy began his speech. "Dearly beloved," he began but Nick interrupted him.

"Wait, I just need to say something first." He turned to Freddy and Joe. "I just want to let you know that I love Mel and I will never hurt her, but more importantly I will never try to trap her or change her. You raised an amazing, beautiful, intelligent woman and I have every intention of encouraging and admiring those qualities for the rest of my life and so..." he hesitated before slowly unbuttoning his pristine white shirt.

Mel frowned, confused as to what he was doing, then more so as Nick began to turn around and then she heard Joe gasp out loud, holding his hand over his mouth.

"What have you done?" she asked, then saw what her father had gasped at.

"I never want you to feel trapped, Mel, but I also never want you to run away from me and so if I ever make you mad or angry, I want you to use this and stay to sort whatever it is that I have done." Mel caught her sobs as she saw her plain, leafless tree that had been tattooed across the whole of Nick's back. The trunk started at the base of Nick's spine and spread upwards, the bare branches reaching out across his shoulders and back. He turned to sneak a glance over his shoulder to see her reaction, tears soaked her cheeks and she turned to walk away. Nick's heart sank, he had pushed her too far, too much too soon, but Mel stopped when she reached his mother.

"Diane," she struggled to speak. "Do you have that lip liner please?" Diane, who was also now crying, reached down into her handbag and handed over the pencil. Mel returned to Nick and turned him away from her. Slowly and delicately she began to draw blossoms, starting at the lowest branch she drew the first one then worked her way up. She only stopped to sharpen the pencil with Joe's penknife when it was blunt, and slowly the tree began to fill up. Nick stood motionless as Mel calmly drew each blossom, hundreds of them, he felt her hand lean against his skin, felt the pencil slowly circle each branch. Each little blossom that she drew on him filled his heart a little more, it wasn't the tree that was blooming anymore, it was his heart she was filling. Each little flower she drew was drawn not out of anger or frustration, but out of love, love for him.

It took over an hour for Mel to finish her drawings but no one minded. Mr Michaels held Diane's hand tightly, and Uncle George choked back tears as he watched the two lovers show the whole village how much they loved one another, the very essence of what a wedding should be. When she finally handed over the pencil, every single person applauded.

"This is how my tree will look every day that I am with you," she confessed to Nick, "You came into my life when I needed you and now I am truly free of my past, I don't want to start my future with anyone else."

"Oh good grief," Billy called out, crying, "Just put your shirt on and let's get you married, I can't stand anymore." Nick laughed and wiped the happy tears from his eyes.

"I don't want to," he said suddenly. "I don't want to smudge it by putting my shirt back on! But I will admit that I am feeling a little self-conscious of everyone looking at me half naked!" He looked into the group of friends and family, frantically looking for a solution.

"That's easily rectified," Freddy shouted out standing up, then began unbuttoning his own shirt.

"Freddy!" Joe called out, mortified.

"No, no, quite right," Uncle George bellowed out loudly and he too began stripping off to the waist, his overly large belly hanging over the top of his trousers. Nick watched astounded as, one by one, all the men in the crowd removed their shirts as the women all giggled. He turned to Freddy, suddenly wanting to hug the man.

"There, you said it was an unconventional wedding, well now it definitely is. Now get on with it and marry my daughter." Freddy sat down again whilst Joe gazed at him dumbfounded.

"Maybe we should all strip off," Nick joked suggestively.

"Are you kidding me? My dad made this dress, I am never taking it off!" Mel cried out proudly. Nick stepped back.

"Joe made this?" He looked over at Joe, who was now embarrassed. "It's beautiful, you are amazing, Joe." Mel laughed. Nick loved her laughter, she was so happy today, she glowed. "Hey maybe we should get your dad to make all our baby clothes," he added, regretting it the minute the words left his mouth as Diane and Joe both sat up shrieking excitedly. "No, no only joking, not yet!" he corrected, "blimey, keen, aren't they," he laughed, as Mel collapsed at the disappointed faces of Diane and Joe.

"Right," Billy began again. "Dearly beloved, we are gathered here today to unite this woman and this beautifully sculpted, muscled..."

"Billy!" everyone called out.

"Alright, I'm sorry," he giggled "...but it is very distracting, you know." Mel leaned over to Nick as everyone was busy laughing at Billy.

"You do want kids, don't you?" she asked, suddenly concerned. Nick smiled and grasped her face into his hands.

"Of course, baby, but you know things cannot be planned..."

"..they just happen," she finished off for him. "Those words sound familiar."

"Yeah, well, they were good advice and they work for us."

"Oh good grief, is this wedding going to happen or what? It is taking all day!" Billy stamped his foot in a huff, causing Uncle George to roar out laughing; even Freddy managed a sly chuckle.

"Right...Where was I? Oh yes...dearly beloved..."

Thank you for taking the time to read Absolute Resolve, if you liked this story please read on for excerpts of other books in The Coffee Café Series, Bitter Reflections and Distinct Desires.

If you would like more information on any of my books please take a look at my website www.crmcbride.co.uk where you can subscribe to receive up to date information on any of my books and be the first to know release dates and read any teasers.

You can also follow me on Twitter @CR_McBride or on Facebook at C.R.McBride.

Thank you

Bitter Reflections

The first book in The Coffee Café Series

SARA ROLLED HER eyes, regretting that she had picked up the damn phone, this was not going to help her mood. Jamie worked at her company, Saltec; it sold and installed computer equipment to companies all over the world. He was one of the company 'geeks', with scruffy black hair and an endless supply of black faded t-shirts, he had been persistently trying to get Sara to go out with him since she asked him for help three months ago.

Not many people ventured into the 'geeks' domain and if they did they never went back again. It wasn't that they were unpleasant, they were all really intelligent people but their social skills were a bit, well lacking, they seemed to speak a whole different language to most people but expected everyone to automatically know what they were on about. If only she'd known that a missing order could cause so much hassle, she wouldn't have bothered chasing it, having to ask him to help her find it, and would have just re-entered it into the system manually.

"Sara! Are you there?" Jamie asked down the line after Sara had not replied, She sighed, unable to keep the frustrated tone from her voice.

"Yes, I'm here, it's just that I am rather busy, Jamie, and to be honest not the best company at the moment."

It was so hard to not upset his feelings but Jamie was about twelve years old, well OK, not twelve but there was no way that he was older than twenty three and with Sara approaching her thirty-fifth birthday there was no way that her sex life had become so depressing that she was going to scrape the bottom of the barrel by becoming a cougar.

"You are mental!" her friend Jo had screeched at her when she had told her about Jamie's advances. "You should totally go for it, it's not like you're getting any from anyone else!"

"Shut up! He's a child; there's no way on earth I am going out with a child, he probably plays computer games all day!" Sara complained.

"You have had no decent man in your life since you left 'The Bastard', Sara, and let's be honest, with the hours you work you hardly fit time in to see me let alone start a relationship!" It was true, Jo was right, she just had no free time whatsoever at the moment, lonely didn't begin to describe how she felt and as for her sex life, it was non-existent. Other than a few thrills from the romance novels that Jo lent her, she had given up on men; Jo, however, moved freely from one guy to the next, never really looking for anything permanent, just someone to have fun with. Sara could never be like that, she had tried it once with a bloke from the coffee shop, Troy, what a disaster. Sara was not fun like Jo, she had been nervous on the date and not interested in him at

all, the night had been a total disaster and after a very weak attempt of seduction on his part and some fumbling Sara had sent him packing and decided quick flings were not for her! Why couldn't she just meet someone like the men out of her books, someone who understood her, who loved her and seduced her passionately but there were no men like that in real life!

"Is he good looking, Sara? If so, you are an idiot for not going for it," Jo insisted.

Mmm, that had been a good question, the truth was she had never really looked at Jamie that way before, she didn't even know his full name. But even still, he was so much younger than her and she was not getting into that, no way.

"Sara, are you still there?" the voice continued.

"Oh God, sorry, Jamie, I went off in a daydream then, yeah I'm fine, just a bit of bad news that's all. Loo,k I really appreciate the offer but Jamie, I just want to be alone tonight."

There was a long pause before he asked almost in a whisper:

"Does that mean that there may be a night when you don't want to be alone?"

Sara couldn't help herself and let out a little giggle, you've gotta love the persistence and eternal hope of youth. She said goodnight and put down the phone, not feeling half as bad as she did before she had picked it up.

Distinct Desire

The third book in The Coffee Café Series

TJ'S HEART RACED as the taxi pulled up outside a huge apartment block across town - the posh end of town, completely at the other end from where she resided. Her eye line was raised as she followed the windows all the way to the top; she could only imagine the views from up there. It had taken her an hour to decide what to wear that morning, jeans seemed too hot for the latest heat wave but a dress was completely out of the question if the deliciously, sexy dreams that she had been subjected through the night were anything to go by. No, she had decided on long shorts, high tops and a plain white vest, very boring, very appropriate.

"Can I help you?" the man sitting behind the desk asked as TJ entered the reception hall of the building.

"Erm, I am here to see Mr Morgan? I'm TJ Knapley."

"Of course, the photographer. Right, I have instructions to give you this key card, this will only open the door to the guest room, which is the door to the left of the main apartment. The interlocking door is locked from both sides, so if it doesn't open for whatever reason then it is locked from the other side." TJ nodded, trying to take in all that he was saying. "I need to see some proof of ID and also I need you to sign here for the key." TJ took the pen from the man's hand and then searched through her purse for her driving licence. He smiled politely, "Right, there is a list of rules in here, no parties, no pets etc etc building house rules and these must be adhered to at all times. So all that is left to do is take the lift on your left up to the top floor, and Mr Morgan will meet you there to give you the lift codes and such. If you would like to leave your luggage here someone will bring it up to you." He offered his hand and she shook it.

"Erm, thank you, but I will take my luggage myself, I appreciate it though." TJ had no intention of leaving all her camera equipment in the hands of a minimum wage baggage handler. Nice or not, it was all too valuable.

She dragged her case to the lift and pressed the highest button, nerves again attacking, causing her to waiver a little as the lift rocked her on its ascent. TJ straightened up her hair that was pulled back into a tight ponytail, then smoothed her shorts down, making sure there were no food stains or coffee stains spoiling the look.

"Ms Knapley, a pleasure to meet you." The man that greeted her was most definitely not Adam Morgan, he was short and round with glasses perched on the tip of his nose, he reached to collect TJs' bag.

"It's OK, I have it, thank you," she offered, reaching for her bag a little too quickly, leaving the man with his hand stretched out in greeting. "Oh I am so sorry," she uttered as she realised and grasped his hand. He smiled a broad wide smile.

"You're not going to be this timid around Adam, are you? I mean, Barbara assured me you would be able to deal with him."

"I am not timid!" TJ defended, standing a little taller. "I am merely ensuring that my cameras get to the location in one piece. I would hate to have to sue Mr Morgan for damages before I have even set foot through the door." She bit her tongue, damn her outburst and in only the first three minutes it had reared its ugly head. The man, however, nodded his approval.

"That's more like it. Please, I assure you I will be very careful with it but if my word is insufficient then I will show you to your room first and you can stash it all away safely." TJ now returned his smile, she did not think he was taking it offensively, and picking up the handle of her case once more she followed him to a small door at the side of the main double doors. Offering her key card to him, he opened the door for her.

"I am Andrew Hasrock by the way, I am Adam's business manager and consultant on all matters business related." He handed her a business card. "If you need anything or have any questions, please let me know, all my contact details are on that card."

"Thanks." TJ took her first look around the room, it was beautiful. Clean white walls were dressed with delicate green fabrics, the largest bed she had ever seen dominated the floor, and there was a small bathroom off to the side. "This is his spare room?"

"Yes, it's lovely isn't it, I have spent many a happy night in here whilst Adam and I have been discussing business until the small hours. Speaking of Adam, I guess we had better get this over and done with." TJ bit her lip, what was it with this guy? Everyone seemed to be petrified of him, how bad could he be? Sucking up her courage, she took a deep breath and followed Andy out of the room. "The connecting doors are locked from both sides, we haven't got over that hurdle yet," he whispered to her, chuckling slightly. "Right, here we go".

As the doors opened so did TJs' mouth, only in the movies had she ever seen a place like this. A complete open plan living area met her eyes first, the wall made up completely of glass, the city displayed like a piece of art before her. Large white sofas were surrounded by oversized green plants and small tables. There was a huddle of people over by the table to the right and they all began to part like curtains, revealing Adam looking at all the paperwork in front of him.

"Adam, this is..." Andy began.

"I know who it is, thank you, there is no need for introductions, Andy." TJ swallowed hard, OK time to turn on the charm.

"Mr Morgan, I would like to thank you for this opportunity to work with you and..." She paused as his crystal blue eyes turned on her, looking her up and down "...erm...well." She tried to re-focus as her mind suddenly went blank. "Well I just wanted to say that I assure you I will be completely professional and will not invade your privacy."

"Your very presence is invading my privacy, Ms Knapley," he snarled and TJ found herself taking a step back.

"Now come on, Adam, we agreed," Andy butted in.

"We agreed nothing - you agreed - you and my mother hatched this scheme up, SHE is nothing to do with me!" Andy was about to complain again when TJ felt a surge of annoyance.

"Now just hold on, Mr, I have just met you, whether you hired me or not the polite thing to do is to return a greeting. Pissed or not. I am sure your mother brought you up better than that!" A gasp could be heard from everyone around him, and again she faltered as Adam rose to his feet.

"My mother!" he repeated. "And what exactly would you know about my mother!"

Unperturbed, TJ stood facing him. "I know enough to know I like her and I do not like you!" she spat. The room was silent, watching the two square off to each other, TJs heart was beating so hard she swore he could see it pounding though her chest as he stood motionless, just staring at her in disbelief.

"I could fire you right now, you know," he counteracted.

"I think we have already established that YOU didn't hire me, your mother did, so you know what, good luck, I'll just wait in my room whilst you phone her and get her to fire me." Confidence was brewing in her veins, she knew his mother had arranged this and there was no way that she was going to let Adam change that. She turned heels and left the stunned room heading towards her little room. She winked at Andy as she passed him, watching him struggling to hide his smile.

"Wait!" Adam called out after her.

TJ stopped and without even turning said, "Giving in already, bloody hell, Adam I was led to believe you would be a challenge. That was just damn right boring. I will go unpack, shall I?" Andy was now holding his sides as TJ slammed the door behind her, and he heard her open her own door, slamming that one for effect.

"It's not funny, Andy," Adam complained.

"No, not at all is it funny, Adam, you getting your arse whipped by a young girl - no definitely nothing funny about that! Excuse me a minute." He walked into the office and Adam heard him let out a large tummy rumbling laugh, his face screwed up in disgust. "Sorry, just had to get that out," he chuckled as he returned. Adam was not amused, he did not like strangers poking their noses into his business, and this one was obviously overly nosy with an attitude to boot. This girl was going to be a nightmare.

TJ sat on the edge of the bed shaking, when Andy gingerly entered.

"Who the hell does that prick think he is?" She was livid that he had made her feel like that; she was here to do a job, not get a ton of abuse for doing it.

"TJ, listen to me, that 'prick' is the reason why you are here and the reason you are getting paid and the reason you will get a heap of work afterwards. I saw you, you can handle yourself, you don't need me to hold your hand in there, so get your arse up and start working." Andy stood up, and before leaving gave TJ a peck on the top of her head. The act shocked her and she looked up at him, he was smiling affectionately and she was helpless to his charm.

"This is going to be a nightmare, isn't it," she muttered.

43809787R00162

Made in the USA
Charleston, SC
07 July 2015